THE HEALING IS HERE . . .

- Betsy Barton remained paralyzed after six years of medical care. Then she discovered Christ. . . .
- A successful businessman lost everything. Then he took a chance on God. . . .
- A prominent newspaper man became a victim of crippling polio. Then he opened his heart to belief. . . .

The Reverend Dr. CHARLES L. ALLEN is pastor to one of America's largest Protestant congregations. More than a million people have read his books; innumerable others have taken inspiration from his radio and TV appearances. His simple, wonder-working faith has brought comfort and renewal to untold numbers of Americans.

The Touch of the Masters' Hand

Christ's Miracles For Today

Charles L. Allen

A JOVE BOOK

THE TOUCH OF THE MASTER'S HAND

A Jove Book / published by arrangement with
Fleming H. Revell Company

PRINTING HISTORY
Eleven previous paperback printings

Jove edition / October 1983

ISBN: 0-515-07378-4

Jove books are published by The Berkley Publishing Group,
200 Madison Avenue, New York, N.Y. 10016.
The words "A JOVE BOOK" and the "J" with sunburst
are trademarks belonging to Jove Publications, Inc.

PRINTED IN THE UNITED STATES OF AMERICA

For my four sisters

Mrs. Heinz M. (Grace) Touraine
ENGLEWOOD, N. J.

Mrs. H. George (Blanche) Bielefelt
LEXINGTON, MASS.

Mrs. Robert F. (Frances) Chamberlain
LONG MEADOW, MASS.

Mrs. Joe G. (Sarah) Wright, Jr.
ANDERSON, S. C.

Contents

THE ARM of Christ is no less than twenty centuries long. That is the amazing truth which sets our hearts to singing with new hope. With great interest we read, "And Jesus, moved with compassion, put forth his hand, and touched him . . ." (Mark 1:41). Physical disease, blindness, disturbed minds, guilt-burdened souls, sorrowful hearts—all were miraculously healed by *The Touch of the Master's Hand*.

The greater miracle is His hand is still reaching out with the same transforming touch. The miracles He once wrought in Galilee are being repeated even now in your town and in my town. I say as the first disciples said, ". . . We speak that we do know, and testify that we have seen . . ." (John 3:11).

The words in this book were not prepared for theoretical classroom discussion, but for my own congregation on Sunday nights at Grace Methodist Church in Atlanta. For more than eight years I have watched the faces of an average of more than a thousand people each Sunday night in that great church. Written in those faces are the same needs that Christ saw in the days of His flesh. At the conclusion of my sermon, I invite those present to walk down the aisle, kneel at the Altar and give Christ a chance to put His hand upon them. Each Sunday night through those eight years an average of not less than *six hundred* people do come and "make their humble confession, meekly kneeling upon their knees."

I put these simple messages in printed form with the

prayer that you who read will also be led to believe, to come to Him, and to experience a miracle within your own life by *The Touch of the Master's Hand*.

CHARLES L. ALLEN

Grace Methodist Church
458 Ponce de Leon Avenue, N. E.
Atlanta, Georgia

1. JESUS WAS NO FROWNING SAINT

The Miracle of Changing the Water into Wine

JOHN 2:1-11

THE MIRACLES of Christ begin at a wedding. That says a lot. Later He used His marvelous power to heal the sick, feed the multitude, quiet the winds and waves and even raise the dead, but the first miracle He wrought was just to keep a happy party from breaking up too soon.

The people of Palestine found very little in life to bring gaiety and laughter. Living for them was hard and meager and very little ever happened out of the ordinary. The most important social event in their lives was a big wedding. Most of their weddings were very simple and quiet but occasionally some family would really put on a big one, and in a little country town like Cana such a wedding would be the social event of the year, probably of several years.

The marriage feast would last for seven days, with fresh guests arriving each day while others went home. Usually the entire town was invited and likely those who weren't invited just came anyway. It began with the bride being led with music in a colorful parade to the home of the bridegroom. Naturally it took a lot of food and wine, and for the host to run short was, of course, very embarrassing.

It is likely that Jesus and some of His disciples had arrived along toward the latter part of the week. Probably His mother had been there for several days and maybe had been helping with the serving. She whispered to Jesus, "They have no wine," and then she told the servants, "Whatsoever he saith unto you, do it." Jesus had the servants fill six waterpots with water. When that was done, He told the servants to draw out some and carry it to the master of ceremonies for the week. Usually the master of the feast was one of the close friends of the bridegroom, perhaps his wedding best man. The master tasted the wine and turned in surprise to the groom saying that it was usual to give the best wine first and save the poorer quality until the last, but he had reversed the order and had kept the good wine until last.

This miracle was the sign of an entirely new relationship between man and God. It put a new meaning into religion. God gave to Moses the power to perform miracles and when he appeared before Pharaoh, his first miracle was a turning of water into blood. It was a symbol of death and destruction. Jesus turned water into wine, a symbol of gladness and rejoicing. His coming was not to condemn and to destroy but to bless and make happy.

Before Jesus was John the Baptist. He was a stern and hard man who exposed the sin of the people and harshly denounced them. He lived unto himself and frowned upon an occasion which brought laughter into people's hearts. John would have been insulted by an invitation to the wedding feast. Certainly he would not have helped to make it a success.

Jesus was different. He came to live with people and to love them. He entered into their daily lives, wept at their funerals and rejoiced with them at their weddings. This first miracle set the tone of His entire ministry. Instead of condemning people, He wanted to give them another chance—"Go, and sin no more" (John 8:11) "Be of good cheer" was an expression often on His lips. For Him, the main activity of God was not a judge but a Father. It is said that St. Théresa disliked "gloomy people" and prayed to be delivered from "frowning saints." She understood the real Christ.

HIS TRANSFORMING POWER

I cannot explain Jesus' miracle of turning the water into wine. If I could explain it I would not regard it as a miracle. But from the evidence I believe that He did it, and because He did it I know certain facts about Him. Jesus commanded that six waterpots be set before Him and then He had the servants fill them with water. Since six large waterpots were as many as a normal household would possess, there likely were no other containers in the house.

So the servants had to go and get the water either from a well or a nearby stream. Anyway, we may be sure that the pots were filled with real water. Jesus Himself did not touch the pots. As soon as they were filled He told the servants to draw some out and carry it to the master of the feast. He tasted it and not only recognized it to be wine, but the very best wine.

Some people have tried to give various explanations seeking to explain away the miracle, but the story is too clear. Through the use of His power, in a moment's flash the water became wine. The disciples were there and saw it happen, and as a result the Bible says, "His disciples believed on Him."

Just a little while before, Jesus was in the wilderness where He was severely tempted by Satan to use His power to turn stones into bread. For forty days He had been without food and He was hungry and weak. But Jesus refused to use His power for His own benefit. Even at the last He said He could pray unto His Father and receive twelve legions of angels (Matt. 26:53). He could have destroyed the entire Roman army, to say

13

nothing of that handful of soldiers who came to take Him, but He refused to do it. Instead, He permitted Himself to be crucified.

But when it came to helping others, He used His power without hesitation. Long before Lloyd C. Douglas wrote *The Robe* and his other famous novels, he wrote a book entitled *Those Disturbing Miracles*. That book is out of print, but I located a copy in a second-hand bookstore in Brooklyn and paid a premium price for it. Much of the book was a disappointment, but this one sentence is worth the price of the book. Speaking of the miracle at the wedding, Lloyd Douglas said: "Surely he is a very unfortunate reader of this epic who gets himself so distracted by all these stone waterpots . . . that he misses the real and only point of issue, which is . . . the simple fact that Jesus bears a transforming power, that He turns water into wine, frowns into smiles, whimpers of fear into anthems of hope, deserts into gardens, and sin-blistered souls into valorous saints by the catalyzing alchemy of a selfless love."

Turning the water into wine is not the important part of this story. No person who believes in God doubts His ability to do that. The real miracle is the fact that Christ, the Son of God, was at the wedding. Who were the people? Nobody knows. They were just ordinary folks like you and me, but Jesus felt at home in their company and they felt comfortable in His presence. He was not aloof and hard to know. He was one of them and entered into their joys and also into their troubles.

And the miracle for me is not what God can do in my own life, but rather what He wants to do and will do if I will accept Him and give Him a chance.

How did Christ change the water into wine at the wedding in Cana? Because it was a miracle we cannot explain it, but from that story we learn that He not only can but will work miracles to help people—even people like you and me. If there is a need or a problem in your life, Christ is concerned. He stands ready and able to help. Of that you can be sure.

Then why is it many people fail to experience His miracle-working power? It is because they do not meet the one requirement. As the condition of His help, He requires from us faith which leads to obedience. His mother said to the servants at the wedding, "Whatsoever he saith unto you, do it." If they had not had faith enough to do what they were told, the miracle never would have been performed.

Before Christ fed the multitude, a little boy gave Him his lunch. Before the sick woman was healed, she touched the hem of His garment. Before the lame man was healed, four men brought him to Jesus. Before the blind man could see, he obeyed the command of Christ to go wash in the pool. Before Christ raised Lazarus from the dead, someone had to roll the stone away from his grave. Before the crippled man at the pool was made whole, he obeyed the Lord, stood and took up his bed.

There is a song which says:

> Trust and obey,
> For there's no other way
> To be happy in Jesus,
> But to trust and obey.

Betsy Barton was paralyzed. For six long years she had sought help and healing but had failed to find it. She was discouraged and had almost lost hope. Then one day she got just the help she needed from the man who lived next door. So often we look for the answer we need in far places when likely we can get the answers right at hand if we will just look for them.

This man knew there were many things she could not do, but he would not listen to those things. We seldom gain help by emphasizing our troubles and weaknesses. One thing Betsy Barton could do was breathe, so this man told her to breathe: "Breathe like this," he said. She had not been breathing as well as she could. Though most of her muscles were paralyzed, not quite all of them were. She could move her stomach muscles so he told her to start moving those.

He said, "Just do these simple things, these innocent things. Do them hard. And let them prove themselves."

Betsy started doing the only two things she could do— breathing and moving her stomach muscles. Later she said, "Upon these two exercises hung my health. With these two simple things as rungs, I started to climb the ladder of strength, to win back my life."

To gain the miracle power of God, you must have enough faith to do what you can. No person's situation is so bad that he cannot do something. I once told a man to pray. He said, "I can't pray. I do not know how." I asked if as a child he learned "Now I lay me down to sleep." He remembered that, so I told him to start with that prayer and say it until he learned how to pray.

On Sunday nights I say to people that even if they can't pray, they can at least walk down the aisle and get on their knees at the altar. When we do what we can do, God will then do what He needs to do. And as a result of what He does, we will find ourselves joining that ever-growing company of His disciples who "believe on Him."

2. HEALING MAY COME THROUGH FORGIVENESS

The Miracle of Healing the Paralyzed Man

MARK 2:1-12

───────────

ONCE JESUS came to Capernaum, probably to rest for a few days. But the word got out that He was there and so many people came to the house where He was that they could not all get in. Many had to stand outside around the doors and windows. Why were people so interested in Jesus? There are several reasons:

(1) Once a leper came and when Jesus saw him He was "moved with compassion" (Mark 1:41). Throughout His ministry we find that He was concerned about the needs of people and He loved them. Never once did He turn his back on any person who came to Him seeking help. When He spoke, people knew He was trying to help them. We are interested in the preacher who is interested in us. As people heard Him they realized: Here is one who is different; He is not trying to get something out of me; He is offering something to me.

Young Joseph Scriven was deeply in love with a young lady. Their marriage plans had been made, but she was drowned. For months he was bitter and discouraged, but out of that experience he became acquainted with the One who could comfort his heart and give him peace. So he wrote:

> What a friend we have in Jesus,
> All our sins and griefs to bear;

What a privilege to carry
Everything to God in prayer.

People loved Jesus, and still do, because He cares.

(2) The crowds came to hear Jesus because He had something important to say. After He had finished the Sermon on the Mount, the Bible tells us the people were astonished at Him "for he taught them as one having authority" (Matt. 7:29). Jesus had the answers for the problems of man and He still has them. Thus we are anxious to hear what He says.

(3) Crowds came to Jesus because He spoke in a language the people could understand. Mark tells us, "The common people heard him gladly" (Mark 12:37). Jesus never tried to impress people with big words, but rather did He express the truth of God so that even the most unlearned would be helped.

(4) Also, great crowds came to hear Christ because no one else could offer what He did. Once He asked His disciples, "Will ye also go away?" Peter replied, "Lord, to whom shall we go?" (John 6:67,68). And that answer still holds. Where is there another who offers to us and to our world what Christ offers? If we should turn our backs on Him, where would we go?

So we are not surprised to read that the people crowded in to hear Him at Capernaum. And we are not surprised that today people still go eagerly where Christ can be found. Though Jesus was tired, He would not turn the people away. He saw their need and did something for them. What did He do? Mark says, "He preached the word unto them." There are some people who feel that preaching cannot help them, so they refuse to listen. But God had only one Son, and He made Him a preacher. Preaching is important.

FOUR MEN WHO REMEMBERED ANOTHER

While Jesus was preaching to the crowd in Capernaum, someone began to tear away part of the roof. Then a bed was lowered from the roof down into the room where Jesus was. That is to me a thrilling part of this story. When the news got around that Jesus was in town, the people rushed to see and hear Him.

In Capernaum was one man who could not go because he was paralyzed. Most of the people forgot him, but there were four men who didn't forget. They took the time and made the effort to go and get this man and bring him to Jesus. I wish we knew the names of those four men. They are the kind of people who delight the heart of God. They not only wanted to see Jesus themselves, they also thought of someone to bring who otherwise could not have come.

Following in the footsteps of those four men is a vast company of consecrated people—those who help to build churches, teachers and workers in the Sunday school, those who sing in the choir, parents who teach their children to pray. In every community there are those who would like to go to church but have no way. Yet vast numbers of church members come with seats in their cars empty. One of the most effective ways to bring someone to Christ is through our prayers. Those four men could not heal their paralyzed friend, but they were willing to bring him to the One who could heal.

Because of the extra time it took to go and get their friend, they arrived late and the house was full. Lesser men would have said, "Well, it's no use," and would have turned back, but these men had ingenuity and persistence and were not to be denied. There is always a way if we will find it. So they climbed on the roof and tore a hole in it so as to get their friend before Christ.

Now comes an important insight into our Lord's

character. A lesser preacher would have resented the disturbance, but not He. He realized that people are more important than sermons. Though He spoke to great crowds, He could always see the individual need. God deals with us not in groups, but one by one. So Jesus stopped His sermon and turned His full attention to this one man who needed help. Now comes the miracle of healing.

First, it was faith that opened the door to Christ's power. "When Jesus saw their faith," it says. Until we express what faith we have, we cannot expect Him to use His power. Maybe the man on the bed did not have faith, but His friends did have it and Jesus accepted that. The church has many responsibilities, but one of its greatest is to keep the faith in a world which has no faith.

Next, Matthew points out that Jesus' first words were, "Son, be of good cheer" (Matt. 9:2). This particular man's trouble was his own fault. It was the result of his sins, but our Lord does not utter one word of condemnation. Instead, Christ gives him hope and inspiration. No matter what our condition is, no matter what the cause, when we come to Christ we find a friendly and encouraging Saviour. The first step in healing the man was to cure his sense of hopelessness.

THE REAL MIRACLE

As Jesus looked at the man who was let down from the roof before Him, He saw his paralyzed legs and He might have said, "Arise, take up thy bed, and walk." Later He did say that, but not at first. He looked deeper to find the cause of the man's paralysis, and in this instance it was something the man had done wrong.

Though few of the details are given, it is not hard to understand this case. The man's wrong had set up within him a guilt fear which had paralyzed him. A mother was telling me recently of seeing her child run out into the street in front of an oncoming car. She wanted to run after the child but she could not move. She could not even cry out to the child. She said she was paralyzed in her tracks. The car stopped and the mother's momentary paralysis was over.

No doubt this man before Christ was in somewhat the same state. Instead of an onrushing car toward his child, he saw the terrible judgment of God bearing down upon him, or maybe it was the shame of a guilty conscience. No one had ever explained to him that he could repent and find forgiveness. Like a black shadow, his wrong had so preyed on his mind that it had made him sick.

A physician said to me that half his patients did not need a drug or an operation, they needed the forgiveness of God. Jesus was the greatest physician of all time and He saw that need in this man. So, instead of saying, "Thy paralysis be healed," He said, "Thy sins be forgiven thee." And that was the real miracle. Even if the man's body had remained crippled, his soul was released from its fear and bondage.

Later, Jesus did heal the man's legs, but not always does He do that. But when we come to Him through faith, He does always do for us that which most needs to be done. Sometimes He lifts the burden; at other times He gives us added strength to bear the burden. Sometimes He changes the circumstances of our lives; at other times He gives us the wisdom to use those circumstances for our own good. Sometimes He makes different the situation which we face; at other times He makes different the person in the situation. In this instance, He healed both the man and his condition.

After the miracle was performed, the people were amazed and said, "We never saw it on this fashion."

They had seen many people trying to help others, but Christ was distinctively different. And He still is. Since He was here in the flesh, we have made marvelous advances in many ways. But people continue to build churches in His name, The Book about Him continues to be the best seller, people still look to Him for something they can find no place else.

How can we explain Christ? He was the greatest teacher and preacher, but there was something more. He was not limited to the physical and psychological methods of healing known to modern science. He understood the spiritual laws of God and He possessed the power of God. Christian faith can do for people what nothing else we know of can do.

3. MUST CHRIST BE PHYSICALLY PRESENT TO HEAL?

The Miracle of Healing the Nobleman's Son

JOHN 4:46-54

A MAN HAD gone twenty-five miles to see Jesus. That was a long way in that day—it was an overnight trip. The Bible described this man as a "nobleman," a man of importance, living a busy life. He would not have taken that trip just out of idle curiosity. Back home his little son was so sick he was "at the point of death."

Under such circumstances the father might have been excused if he had sent one of his servants or asked one of the neighbors to make the trip for him. Surely this father wanted to stay close to his son's bedside at such a time. At any moment the little fellow might pass away.

Doubtless his wife needed his help and the comfort of his presence just then.

Somehow the news reached him that Jesus was in Cana. When he heard that he immediately set out for that little town, and when he found the Lord he asked Him to come and heal his son. The Bible says he "besought" Christ, which is a stronger word than "asked." The word "besought" implies pleading, urgency, persistence.

It indicates that the father was convinced of two things: first, that there was a definite need; second, that Christ could meet that need. Add those two convictions together and they result in prayer. No person really prays until he has a need that his own strength and resources seem insufficient to meet. As long as we can take care of ourselves, prayer is a meaningless experience to us.

Yet there are vast numbers who have desperate needs but never really pray. Why? Because they do not actually believe that any real help would come from God. Vast numbers of people are practical atheists. They intellectually believe in the existence of a God, but not to the extent that they count on God to take a hand in the affairs of their own lives. Thus, if we do not believe God can or will help us, we see no need of praying.

The other day I was talking with someone in my study when a telephone call came through from another state. After I hung up my friend asked what it was about and I told him the call was a request for prayer. He felt the person was silly to spend several dollars on a call merely asking for prayer. Yet this man in Jesus' day felt it was worthwhile to leave the bedside of a very sick child and make a day's journey to ask the help of Christ. I admire his faith. He had more faith than many people today, in spite of twenty centuries of Christian history.

23

Of course, Jesus heard his prayer and He answered it. God hears every prayer. God answers every prayer. Remember, I said *prayer,* and I have pointed out that fundamental to prayer is a sense of need that we ourselves cannot meet, and faith that God is both able and willing to meet that need. Sometimes we merely repeat pious words and phrases. I repeat: God hears and answers every *prayer.*

HE GIVES THE RIGHT ANSWER

Because his child was sick and because he believed Christ could heal that child, a certain nobleman traveled twenty-five miles to ask Christ's help. Christ heard and He responded to the man's plea. In every instance, when the plea for help was sincerely made, Christ answered. But His answers were not always given in the same way. Sometimes His answer is in a different way than we wanted or expected, but His is always the right answer in the right way.

We remember how Jairus came to Christ in an almost exact circumstance. His daughter was at the point of death and he prayed Christ to come and lay His hands upon her. Without a word, Jesus immediately went with him to his home, stood by the girl's bedside and brought her back to health (Mark 5:22-43).

On the other hand, word came one day that His dear friend, Lazarus, was sick. His sisters were so anxious for Jesus to come. Yet He waited two days before He did anything. In fact, it seemed He waited too long. Lazarus died and was buried before Jesus made any answer to their prayer. Yet, if we read the story all the way through, we find that He never lost control of the situation (John 11). Let us learn well the lesson of prayer: faith makes its plea and then leaves the how and the when of the answer in God's hand.

This nobleman who came to Christ had more faith than a lot of people have today, and yet his faith was limited. He believed that the actual physical presence of Christ was necessary for the working of His miracles, so he did not content himself with putting his need before Christ, trusting the Lord would decide best how to meet it. Instead, the man insisted that Christ come to his home.

We see evidences of that same limited faith today. Walk down the street and ask the people you meet, "Do you believe Christ actually performed miracles?" The overwhelming majority will say "Yes." Most of us do not question that fact that He made the crippled walk, the blind see, the sick well. We accept without hesitation the fact that the winds and the waves obeyed His voice.

Ask those same people, "Do you believe Christ can and will work those same miracles today?" Usually you will get a stammering reply of double talk. Rarely will you get a clear-cut answer of "Yes." Most people do not believe that Christ will work a miracle in their very own lives.

Ask the same people, "If Christ were here today in the flesh, do you believe He could and would work the miracles like unto those when He was in Galilee?" Again, most people would immediately say "Yes." The conclusion is clear: most people today really feel that the physical presence of Christ is necessary to the expression of His power.

The disciples believed that, even when He died. They gave up and quit. But when He ascended they had learned differently, and they went out to turn a world upside down in His Name. Those men learned the essential lesson of the Christian faith—Christ is not dead. He is a living power in the lives of men.

BELIEVE IN THE ANSWER

"Go thy way; thy son liveth." That was Christ's answer to a desperate man's prayer. His son was sick unto death. He left his bedside and traveled twenty-five miles to see Christ. He had prayed the Lord to come to his house and heal the boy. Notice very carefully the father's prayer. He did not ask Christ to heal his son, he asked Christ to come to his house and heal his son. At this point we are dealing with the very essence of the Christian faith.

Suppose your own child was about to die and you went for a physician. And suppose when you told him of your need, he merely told you to go on back home and your child would be all right. You would be deeply offended. You would rush in search of another physician. You would expect this father to feel offended at Christ.

But there was something the man saw in Christ that convinced him. He learned the lesson, and the story reads: "The man believed the word that Jesus had spoke, and he went his way." In fact, so convinced was he that his prayer was answered that he became relaxed and at ease. He did not rush back home that night. There was no need for that. He knew so well that everything would be all right that he went and found a bed and rested.

Jesus told us, "What things soever ye desire when ye pray, believe that ye receive them, and ye shall have them" (Mark 11:24). The faith to pray is only half enough. We must also have the faith to believe the answer has been given. In *Grace Abounding,* John Bunyan confesses that one abomination of his own heart is that he has not watched for the answers to his prayers. We would not be so discourteous as to ask a favor of a friend but then turn away without even hearing his answer. When we pray, we must believe God has answered.

On the way home the next day the man saw his servants coming to meet him. They were worried about him now. He had frantically gone in search of help. He had not come home that night so they were going in search of him. The servants told him the boy was all right. The man was not surprised. He merely inquired at what hour the boy got better. They told him the fever left the boy "yesterday at the seventh hour." The father remembered that was the exact hour Jesus had spoken. The miracle had been performed—the lesson was learned. His power is not dependent on His physical presence.

So often we talk about the second coming of Christ as if He is helpless until then. My dear friends, Christ is here now. That is what makes the Christian faith so different from every other religion. Our Lord is not One who merely once lived and told us how to live. He lives now. The Christian shrine is not at a grave in some garden. That grave is empty—deserted.

When He ascended into heaven, the disciples did not feel left alone. As Dr. Malty said, "It was expedient that He go out of some men's sight in order to be near to all men's hearts." Whatever your need, He can meet it. His power is sufficient.

Oh what peace we often forfeit,
Oh what needless pain we bear,
All because we do not carry
Everything to God in prayer!

4. HOW TO GET CHRIST'S GREATEST BLESSING

The Miracle of Healing Ten Lepers

LUKE 17:12-18

THE STORY begins: "And as he entered into a certain village, there met him ten men that were lepers"—ten wretched, forsaken men. Leprosy in that day was a hopeless disease, as hopeless as death. In fact it was death, except that just a part of you died every day. Maybe today a finger would die. Later a toe or even a foot would be gone. An ear would drop off. It was a gruesome disease. There was no way to treat it. Since it was contagious, the leper was driven out of society.

In their leprosy they formed a fellowship. Likely these men had not been friends in life but their common suffering had now brought them together. That frequently happens. I have seen married couples drawn close to each other through some suffering or sorrow. Many of our unhappiest marriages are the ones where there have been no struggles and hardships. My wife and I have a little penny bank that means a lot to us. In our first year together we put our pennies in the little bank. Then would come a time, rather frequent times, when all we had were the pennies, and carefully we would count them out to buy the few things we couldn't get along without. But it was a lot of fun.

You have missed life itself if you cannot think of some person or group as you sing the old hymn:

We share each other's woes,
Each other's burdens bear,
And often for each other flows,
The sympathizing tear.

Some people insist on going it alone. They do not make friends. They refuse to belong to a church. But there is creative power in fellowship, especially the fellowship of suffering. Even lepers found it so.

One of them had heard about Jesus. He told the others and little by little hope rose up in their hearts. They reached the point of believing. It is much easier to build up your faith with others than by yourself. That is why we have the organized church. The experience of the centuries has taught us that though people possibly can maintain their faith alone, it is much harder that way. Even in spite of leprosy, these men were determined to live.

There is a marvelous lesson here for those who are discouraged, for those who see no hope in the future, for those who would quit. Those people need the strengthening power of a fellowship. It may take time and effort, but it is worth it. I say to people who join a church, "It takes only a little time to put your name on the roll, but to become really a member of the church will take longer. It requires working with the people and becoming one of the many." Fellowship with others requires the giving of much but eventually it means the getting of much.

Through fellowship with each other even a group of lepers found the inspiration and strength to keep trying.

FAITH PLUS OBEDIENCE

When the ten lepers met Jesus they said, "Master, have mercy on us." I like their faith. There are some

29

people who don't believe in prayer. They see others going to the altar but that is not for them. They have needs in their lives they cannot meet, but they give up and quit instead of praying. These ten lepers had faith enough to believe that Christ could do something even about their situation.

Jesus said, "All things are possible to him that believeth" (Mark 9:23). The only limit to the power of God in our lives is the limit of our belief. In this instance of the ten lepers, Jesus saw fit to test out their faith. He did not always do that. On another occasion a leper came to Christ and immediately he was healed (Mark 1:40-45). But sometimes our faith needs to be perfected along the road of obedience.

So Jesus said to these men: "Go show yourselves unto the priests." They might have looked at themselves and each other. They had experienced no change. They had not felt anything. But sometimes God answers our prayers on condition that we exercise our faith. Instead of turning away disappointed, these ten men did what He said. We remember the song, "Trust and Obey." Sometimes the obeying takes more faith than the trusting.

Now notice, "And it came to pass, that, as they went, they were cleansed." We have problems and needs. We sincerely pray, but the full answer is not given us and we are disappointed. But God always gives enough strength for the next step. He always tells us something we can do. Maybe it isn't much but at least we have enough to start. As the children of Israel journeyed through the wilderness, God sent only enough bread for each day, but they gathered that and pressed on, until one day they did possess their Promised Land. Usually God answers our prayers "as we go."

Can you imagine anything more wonderful than suddenly being cured of leprosy? It happened simultaneously to these ten men. Together they had suffered, together they had prayed, together they were healed, together they went joyfully forward. That is, all except one. One of them thought of Christ again; one of them turned back to find Him again; one of them still felt the need of prayer; one of them received Christ's greatest blessing.

What is it we want of God—a house, an automobile, some money in the bank, food to eat and clothes to wear, physical health? Surely we want that and God wants us to have it. He grows trees to make lumber; He puts metals in the earth to make automobiles; He put fertility in the soil to grow our food. Within the world He created there are cures for every disease, and one by one men are finding them. When we get these things, are we satisfied and have we no further need for God? In this story, nine out of ten were satisfied just to be healed.

ONE REMEMBERED TO THANK

Ten lepers went to Christ for healing; only one returned to thank. Ten went to ask; only one came back to praise. Why did the nine fail to thank Christ for His blessing? Why do we fail to thank? There are several reasons.

Pride, conceited pride, is the greatest reason for the thanklessness of man. Do you remember the rich farmer Jesus told about? He made abundant crops, but those crops did not cause him to think of the One who created the soil and sent the sunshine and rain. It only caused him to think of how he could enjoy himself.

In my mind I can hear these ten lepers talking as they rushed back to their home towns: "They thought leprosy would kill me but I whipped it. You can't keep a good man down." It is so easy to blame all our failures on somebody else and all our successes on ourselves. And that doesn't make for gratitude. We are never thankful for what we have earned. When you get your pay check you don't write a note of thanks to the boss. More probably you feel like telling him off for not paying you what you are worth.

To be thankful means that we must admit that we have received more than we deserved. Gratitude comes from a sense of unworthiness. The Bible tells us to humble ourselves, but instead we like to boast and to promote ourselves, and we like to use our blessings to feed our conceit and to support our pride. That is why we are not thankful.

Also, we are not thankful because we concentrate on our troubles instead of on our blessings. These nine lepers had suffered both in body and in mind. There were financial reverses, the loss of friends. It is so easy to let past trouble kill all the joy of today and tomorrow. A line from Lew Wallace's great book, *Ben Hur,* tells us: "In thankfulness for present mercies nothing so becomes us as losing sight of past ills." But some people never learn to forget and go forward. Instead of gratitude for the good, they are only bitter over some bad. There life stops for them and they become dead souls.

This one leper recognized that he had received answer to his prayer. He, too, had a home and family he was anxious to get back to. He, too, had a business that needed his attention. But also, he was a decent man. Something had come to him that he had not earned nor deserved. He had come praying, "Master, have mercy," and through mercy, not justice, he was blessed. Now he recognized that and was big enough to express gratitude.

When Jesus saw him coming back alone He said, "Were there not ten cleansed? but where are the nine?" The Lord was very disappointed; not disappointed because He wanted their praise, but rather because He had an even greater blessing that He could not give the other nine. To the one man with the faithful heart He said, "Arise, go thy way: thy faith hath made thee whole."

Many people have possessed His physical blessings, but they are not happy and in their hearts is no peace. But for those who recognize their blessings and express their gratitude there is a spiritual wholeness awaiting, which is Christ's greatest blessing.

5. THE SIX STEPS OF THE GOSPEL

The Miracle of Healing Blind Bartimeus

MARK 10:46-52

THERE ARE six main steps in the Christian gospel. We see each of them clearly illustrated in the story of Jesus and Bartimeus. First, there is the need. In this case it was physical blindness. "Blind Bartimeus sat by the highway side begging," the story says, and immediately our hearts go out to him.

Of all our physical faculties, we probably cherish the ability to see the most. We would rather lose our hearing, or our ability to speak, or even our arms or legs than to lose our sight. To help us to see more we have developed the microscope and the telescope. We have spent millions and millions on motion pictures, and now television is becoming one of our largest industries. We like to see, and we sympathize with one who is blind. I heard of a blind man on the corner with his tin cup that stopped nearly every passer-by. About his neck was a sign reading, "It is May and I am blind."

But there are needs even greater than physical sight. In his novel, *The Nazarene*, Sholem Asch imagines a blind man mocking Jesus and the Lord replies, "What shall it avail if thou art made seeing with thine eyes and thy heart remaineth blind?" People who have let hate, greed, selfishness or something else blind their hearts are in even greater need. The need might be the burden of a guilty conscience, or the loss of a reason for living, or a broken heart, or some depressing fear or some other need.

Because of that need in our lives that we ourselves cannot meet, we feel that life is passing us by. Bartimeus was not out in the procession marching with his fellows. He sat by the highway side—he was on the sideline. Maybe he had become afflicted with an even worse need in that he had given up and become resigned to his place. He could see no better days ahead —he had grown hopeless. Whatever our need, realizing it is the first step of the Christian gospel.

Second, is the awakening of our belief in Christ and our desire for Him. Doubtless some passer-by said to Bartimeus, "Why don't you get up from the sideline of life and make yourself count for something?" Pitifully he replied, "Don't mock me. You know I would, except I am blind. I cannot do anything."

In my imagination I hear the man's reply: "There is a man named Jesus, of the house of David. He has been doing marvelous things for people. He caused the daughter of Jairus to live again, he fed five thousand people with one little boy's lunch, he healed ten lepers, he quieted the wild man who lived in the cemetery, he has caused deaf men to hear and even blind men to see."

That is the best news Bartimeus has ever heard. Hope begins to rise in his heart, a desire to meet this Jesus takes possession of him, and he begins to feel the thrill of a new expectancy. First, we must realize our need. Second, we must believe Christ can meet that need.

THE PRAYER THAT STOPPED CHRIST

One day as blind Bartimeus sits by the highway side, he hears a multitude approaching. Someone calls the name of Jesus, and the blind man's heart begins to leap within him. Jesus, the One who can cause him to see, the One who can meet his need is now nearby. Bartimeus begins to cry out, "Jesus, thou son of David, have mercy on me."

That is the third step of the Christian gospel—we must ask for Christ's help. Jesus told us, "And all things whatsoever ye shall ask in prayer, believing, ye shall receive" (Matt. 21:22). The limit He places is not on His ability or willingness to give, but on our willingness to ask and our capacity to believe. No greater moment comes into the life of any person than when, out of a recognition of need and faith in Christ's power to meet that need, he falls on his knees in humility and begins to pray.

Notice the prayer of this blind man. He prays without apology. There are some people around who try to stop him, but he pays no attention. There are always some to scoff at the power of prayer and there is always danger of being so concerned about what others might think that we miss its blessing. But Bartimeus is only concerned about his need and the power of Christ to meet that need, and when someone tries to stop him, the Bible says "he cried the more a great deal."

And what does he pray? He doesn't try to explain that his blindness is no worse than somebody else's. He doesn't try to excuse himself. "Have mercy upon me," he says. That is all, and that was enough. Christ can always tell when one is sincere and when the prayer comes really from the heart.

"And Jesus stood still," we read. That is the fourth step. What a marvelous revelation of God that is! In company with a multitude, Christ was bent on some mission. But above the noise of the crowd He heard the cry for help, and He stopped. Prayer has the power to stop God and center His attention upon you—just you. Suppose this blind man had not prayed? Christ would have passed him by. And how many needs are there in your life that are not met simply because you have not prayed? How many times has God passed you by because you did not ask Him to stop?

This man whose prayer stopped Christ was not the ruler of the country, not some very prominent or influential person; he was a mere beggar. He was a man who was on the very bottom rung of the social ladder. But in the face of the need of just one obscure person, the Son of God stopped and to him gave His full attention and made available His mighty power.

As pastor of a church on a main thoroughfare in a big, overcrowded city, I have come to realize that there are vast numbers of people who are lonely, wretched and lost. Our thinking is concerned with the masses; we forget the one person. But not Christ. He knows us one by one and when we call, He hears and returns that call. So we can sing with confidence:

> Pass me not, O gentle Saviour,
> Hear my humble cry;
> While on others thou art calling,
> Do not pass me by.

OLD COATS TO THROW AWAY

Now notice the fifth step in that story: "And he, casting away his garment, rose, and came to Jesus."

His garment—probably an old coat he had. It was not wrong for him to have it and no doubt he enjoyed wearing it. But in this instance that coat was a hindrance. By holding on to the coat he could not get to Christ as easily and as quickly. So without hesitation he cast it aside. It is at this point so many fail. We do want Christ, but there are some other things we are unwilling to let go. It may be some positive wrong that we hesitate to give up. It may be something that is good, but it takes our time and attention and keeps us away from Him. As long as there is anything which you are not willing to surrender, you cannot possess the power of the Saviour.

Sin and sinful habits is one of the coats we must cast aside. He said, "Blessed are the pure in heart: for they shall see God" (Matt. 5:8). Whatever wrong I have done, He stands ready and able to forgive it, but even He cannot forgive until I forsake it. When you kneel to pray, is there something that stands between you and God? If so, turn it loose and trust Him to give you the strength necessary to overcome it.

The love of ourselves is another garment we must cast aside if we would come to Christ. He said, "He that loseth his life for my sake, shall find it" (Matt. 10:39). As long as we are concerned only for ourselves and what we can get out of life, we can never possess Him who died that others might live. Consecration is the pathway to His power.

There are other hindrances in our progress toward Christ: the fear of what other people might think, the shrinking from the discipline of the Christian life, the fear that we could not live up to our Christian decision, the substitution of our gifts and services for the gift of ourselves, or it may be something else in our lives.

St. Paul went even further. Not only was he willing to give up that which hindered his spiritual progress, he even cast it aside if it hindered someone else. He said: "Wherefore, if meat causeth my brother to stumble, I will eat no flesh for evermore, that I cause not my brother to stumble" (I Cor. 8:13). We must recognize the importance of our influence.

The thing to remember is that Christ is never willing to take second place with us. We must put Him first and desire Him to the extent that for Him we are willing to give up anything, even everything, or else we will never have Him.

The story of Bartimeus ends: "And immediately he received his sight, and followed Jesus in the way." That is the final step. He got what he needed, he got off the sideline, he began to live again. It was a miracle, but one that Christ can repeat in the life of any person today.

6. FOUR STEPS TO FAITH

The Miracle of Healing the Centurion's Servant

LUKE 7:1-10

How DOES a person get faith? We have the story of a man who had such complete faith that even Christ marveled at it and proclaimed it the greatest faith He had found in all Israel (Luke 7:1-10). We have many instances recorded when Christ was surprised at the unbelief and lack of faith in people, but this is the only time when He found an even greater faith than He expected. The man and his faith are worthy of our study.

He was a centurion, an officer in the Roman army. His beloved servant was so sick he was about to die. This officer heard that Jesus was in his community, so he sent his friends to Him asking that He heal the servant. No doubt Christ was very busy, but He was never too busy to hear and to respond to a call of human need. He is not too busy today to hear those who need and want Him.

A MAN UNWORTHY

As He came near to the man's house, the centurion sent word to Christ asking Him not to go to the trouble actually to come into his house. First, he felt himself unworthy. He said, "I am not worthy that thou shouldst enter under my roof." Second, he felt it unnecessary for Christ to come in person. He said, "Say in a word, and my servant shall be healed." Those are two basic conditions upon which we receive the power of Christ.

A man said to me recently, "After what I have done, I have no right to pray or to expect God's help." I said, "That is certainly true and it is wonderful that you realize it." No person is worthy of the goodness of God. The most hopeless person is the one who feels he can buy the favor of God through good works. The Bible tells us: "By grace are ye saved through faith; and not of yourselves; it is the gift of God: Not of works, lest any man should boast" (Ephesians 2:8, 9). In that passage the meaning of grace is undeserving mercy.

None of us are deserving. All of us are in the position of the son who said, "I am no more worthy to be called thy son" (Luke 15:21). We all need to stand by the side of the penitent publican in the temple and pray with him, "God be merciful to me a sinner" (Luke

18:13). The Psalmist told us: "The sacrifices of God are a broken spirit: a broken and a contrite heart" (Ps. 51:17).

Before we take the Sacrament of the Lord's Supper in my own church, we pray, "We do not presume to come to this thy table, O merciful Lord, trusting in our own righteousness, but in thy manifold and great mercies. We are not worthy so much as to gather up the crumbs under thy table." Realizing our own unworthiness and trusting in God's compassionate mercy, we can ask His help.

I like the words of the hymn:

> Let not conscience make you linger;
> Nor of fitness fondly dream.
> All the fitness He requireth,
> Is to feel the need of Him.

PHYSICAL PRESENCE OF CHRIST NOT NECESSARY

The centurion, whose servant was sick unto death, said to Jesus, "Say in a word, and my servant shall be healed." He realized that it was not necessary for Christ to be physically present with the man. He went on to say, "For I also am a man set under authority, having under me soldiers: and I say unto one, Go, and he goeth; and to another, Come, and he cometh; and to my servant, Do this, and he doeth it."

Being a trained officer in the army, he recognized the meaning of power and authority and he realized that Christ was a man of authority and power in the realm of the spirit. This centurion could issue a command and it set in motion the operation of certain laws of the government. So Christ could speak and there would be set into operation certain spiritual laws of the universe.

This servant who was sick probably did not know

Christ. Surely he did not know anyone had petitioned Christ on his behalf. No doubt the sick servant was unconscious. Yet Christ did speak the word and the servant was healed. Here a very important truth of intercessory prayer is made clear. Christ always worked His miracles as a result of faith, but it was not necessary always for the person to be helped to have faith.

We remember how James said, "The prayer of faith shall save the sick" (James 5:15). There the faith required was not in the sick but rather in the person praying. Of course, if the sick person also expresses faith along with the one praying for him that is all the better. But it is not always essential. The same is true in reference to praying for any need of another. If we pray with proper faith, though the other person may seem completely indifferent to God, our prayers can bring great results.

Never a day goes by that I do not get requests for prayer. These I take very seriously, and over a period of years I have seen so many results from prayer that I now have much faith in it. When I pray for a person, first I try to fix clearly in my mind that person. Then I seek in my mind a clear picture of Christ, concentrating on just those two together. Then I imagine there is some reason why that person does not take hold of the healing hand of Christ. If that person had the faith he should have, he would probably not need my prayers. So I seek to substitute my own faith for his lack of faith and I think of my own prayers as lifting him or her into actual contact with Christ.

I cannot explain the laws of prayer and exactly how they operate. Neither can I explain the laws by which television works, but I do know I can sit in my home and by television, watch a program in New York. Because I do not understand television is no reason why I cannot use it. The same may be said for the power of prayer. I have seen so many answers to prayer that now I do not doubt that somehow one person's prayers can change the life or physical condition of another person, even if the other person has no faith—even if the other person does not know about the prayers on his behalf.

Jesus healed the servant because of the faith of the centurion.

HIS FOUR STEPS TO FAITH

As far as we know, Jesus marveled at the faith of only this one man. How did this man get his faith? He was not born into a home of faith and he was not trained in his early childhood. For many of us, faith comes normally and naturally because of the training we received by godly parents and teachers. But this man's faith came in other ways. As I read the story, it appears to me there were four main steps to his faith:

(1) He became acquainted with Christ. We are not actually told that in the story, but if that had not been true, then he would not have sought Christ's help. Maybe he met Christ personally. Maybe he heard about Him and went to hear Him preach or to see Him perform His miracles. Surely this soldier was not trained in theology but somewhere, somehow, he came to know Christ.

I have asked a number of people to read carefully and thoughtfully one of the four Gospels ten times. I urge them not to think about the meaning of every verse, but rather to get well acquainted with the One who is written about. One reading is not sufficient. We need to spend much time in company with another in order to get to know him, and I have found that ten careful readings of one of the gospels does give one sufficient time to get acquainted with Christ. And to know Him is to believe in Him.

(2) This centurion supported the church. The Jews said, "He hath built us a synagogue." When a person gets interested in the church and works to build it, eventually he comes to believe in Him who is the foundation of the church. Just recently I have seen the congregation of which I am pastor put a lot of money and effort into enlarging their church building. Not only did they enlarge their building, they also enlarged their own faith. The church has its flaws, but it is still the greatest faith-building institution on earth.

(3) This centurion was a man of humility. He says, "I am not worthy that thou shouldst enter under my roof." A conceited person never finds Christ. And what is worse, he never even desired to find Him. As long as we feel that we can get along by ourselves, we don't need faith in Christ. Faith is developed out of our realization of our own weakness. Each Sunday night I invite people to kneel at the altar to pray. I know one can pray sitting in the pew, but I also know it helps to get on our knees.

(4) This man believed in other people. We see his concern for the servant who was sick. We know he was interested in people or else he would not have built them a church. And the very fact that he was seeking to help others indicates that he believed they were worth helping. We read that God made man "in his own image" (Gen. 1:27). So, if we learn to believe in people, we naturally believe in God. On the other hand, if we are critical of others and hold spirits of envy or ill will in our hearts, then naturally we feel the same way toward God.

Those are four steps to faith. Walk them and you yourself will marvel at what faith does for you.

7. THIRTY-EIGHT YEARS IS A LONG TIME

*The Miracle of Healing the Man
at the Pool of Bethesda*

JOHN 5:1-9

IN ST. JOHN'S gospel there is a story about a man who had been sick for thirty-eight years. I feel a real sympathy for that man. Thirty-eight years is a long time. We can imagine that when he first got sick his friends came to see him, brought him flowers and food and sought to cheer him up.

If he had died, they would have grieved for him and attended his funeral. If he had gotten well his friends would have congratulated him. But since he neither died nor got well, likely their visits became less frequent and after awhile there were no flowers in his room. As the weeks grew into months and the months into years, it is likely the poor fellow was pretty much forgotten. Some of his friends moved away, others died. If he had any children, they grew up and made their own homes. Probably his wife died. And now, after thirty-eight years of sickness, he was alone.

But he refused to give up. In Jerusalem, down by the sheep market, there was a pool that had a strange healing power. The people believed that from time to time an angel would come and trouble the water. The first sick person to get into the water would then be healed. This man somehow got to the pool and faithfully he watched for the times when the water was troubled. Each time he would make an effort to get in, but always somebody beat him to it. Surely, the repeated disappointments must have been hard to bear.

DO YOU WANT TO BE WELL?

Other sick people around the pool had members of their family or friends to help them, but this poor fellow had nobody. So naturally they would beat him into the water, but he refused to give up. He stayed there and kept trying. One day Jesus saw him and asked, "Wilt thou be made whole?" That is, do you really want to get well?

That is the most important question to ask any sick person. Many people really want to be sick. Leslie Weatherhead tells of a woman who was informed by her doctor that she had an incurable cancer. But later it was discovered she did not have cancer at all. She refused to leave the hospital and was more upset by being told that she was well than that she was dying. She said, "I cannot bear the thought of facing life again."

When one reaches the point that life is hard to bear, being sick is one way of escape. I have known people who had not received the love and attention they desired and to get it, they got sick. Many sick people do not want to be well.

We lose patience and treat with contempt that type of sickness. We use the term "neurotic" with a sneer. We have no sympathy with sickness when we decide it is merely in the person's mind. However, that is the sickest sickness of all and the very hardest to cure. In this story we see how Jesus cured it.

Jesus asked, "Wilt thou be made whole?"—do you want to get well? That very question of Christ's implies that He believed the man was really sick. He did not say, "You are not sick, quit pretending." Though this man's sickness was in his mind, still it was a real sickness —the worst sickness.

Also, in the question of Christ's is implied the possibility of a cure. To have asked the man if he wanted to get well when there was no hope for him would have been cruelty. Clovis Chappell says it would be like saying to a hungry man at your door, "Would you like a good dinner?" and then slamming the door in his face; or saying to a drowning man, "Would you like to be saved?" and then leaving him in the water.

But even Christ could not heal the man against his will. There is no limit to what God can and will do for us when we really want Him to. First, we must want it. The man at the pool really wanted to be healed, but the conditions never were right for him. He could not quite make it to the water at the proper time.

How many people have I known who were wasting their lives waiting for the right conditions. We are going to do wonderful things, we are going to be the person we want to be—sometime. But it never is quite the right time. Anytime is the right time when our will is in harmony with God's will.

RISE

So Jesus says to the man, "Rise." That was a strange command. This man was paralyzed. The one thing he could not do was rise. Christ always challenges us with what seems to us our impossibility. And amazing it is what we can do in His power. In the presence of Christ the man actually did rise. I have seen it happen many times. On the Sunday nights during the past several years I have seen many more than a hundred thousand people kneel at the altar of the church and pray. I could name literally hundreds who have later told me of marvelous strength and changes in their lives that came to them there. By ourselves our will power is insufficient, but Christ is so great that in His presence His will becomes our will, and we realize with St. Paul: "I can do all things through Christ which strengtheneth me" (Phil. 4:13).

In Tennessee, recently, a man came to the hotel to see me. He said he wanted to ask my opinion of divine healing. I asked why he wanted to know. He told me that for years he had been sick. He carried pills in nearly every pocket. Then he began to pray and study his Bible and he said, "Now I don't take any pills at all and I feel good."

I said, "My opinion of divine healing is not important to you. What really matters is that through the power of Christ you have been made whole." How that power comes is not my greatest concern. The thing that counts is that when a man finds Christ, he has strength he never had before.

TAKE UP THY BED

After Jesus told the paralyzed man at the pool of Bethesda to rise, He next told him, "Take up thy bed." That is, do everything possible to eliminate your temptation to fall back into your old way.

Little by little the life to which we become accustomed takes hold of us, and though we have longings and hopes of a better way, the ties of the old way are hard to break. This man had depended on his pallet for so long that if he had left it within reach, its pull on him would have been stronger than the pull of the new life.

When a person makes a new decision or resolution, one of the most strengthening things he can do is to tell somebody about it. I remember how my father used to preach for decisions, and then he would make what the old preachers used to call a "proposition." They would say, "If you will make this decision, while we sing a hymn come down and give me your hand." Preachers do not do that much now but it had real value. A public profession is one way of taking up your bed.

When you stand in the strength of Christ, don't think about the possibility of falling. We remember how Peter walked on the water as long as he kept looking at Christ. When he began to look at the winds and waves, he began to sink.

WALK

After the paralyzed man stood and took up his bed, Jesus told him to "Walk." That is, begin some activity. I think the most redeeming institution on the face of this earth is the church. I believe so strongly in the worth of the church that I am investing my entire life in its service, doing what I can to get others to become part of the church.

Yet the church has many critics. Some of the critics are outside the church. They do not worry me because I just stay away from those. The ones I do worry about are those whose names are on the roll but it means nothing to them. Like the man at the pool, they complain that nobody will help them. They complain, "The preacher never comes to see me—I go, but nobody shakes hands with me—the church is after my money—I don't like the music—too many members of the church are hypocrites—" and so forth.

But I have noticed that when the complaining fellow begins to walk on his own within the church—to support the church with his prayers, his presence, his gifts and his service—he finds joy and strength therein. One is "made whole" only when he begins some worthwhile activity. The sickest people are usually those who have the least to do.

One thing more. Later on, probably the next Sunday, Jesus found in the temple this man who had been healed. I like to believe he went to give thanks to God for his healing. Once Jesus healed ten lepers, but only one came back to thank Him. And in the expressing of his thanks he received an even greater blessing. God has done wonderful things for us—don't forget to come back to express your appreciation.

8. THE TOUCH THAT HEALS

The Miracle of the Woman Who Touched the Hem of His Garment

MARK 5:25-34

"DAUGHTER, thy faith hath made thee whole," said Jesus. That is the only time Jesus ever used the term "daughter" in addressing another person. As you read the New Testament, you are impressed with the tenderness He expressed so often toward those in need. He was always kind and gentle toward those who sought His help. But toward one person He seemed to feel a loving sympathy that He never felt toward any other. "Daughter," He said, just that one time.

Let's look at the story and get acquainted with the person. Jesus was on His way to restore to health a little girl. A great crowd was following to see Him perform a miracle. Some were merely curious. Some were hoping He would fail. Others were declaring He had the power. But in the crowd was one woman who was different.

For twelve years she had suffered with what was probably a bleeding cancer. They knew nothing of radium and X-ray in that day. Surgery was a very crude

49

thing and it was used to little advantage. They knew nothing of the wonderful pain-relieving drugs that we have today. She had gone to many physicians, but no one had helped and she had grown steadily worse. On her face was written pain and weakness and worry. Now she had spent every cent she had and was at the point of desperation.

I don't know the woman's name nor her station in life. She could have been anybody. Pain, suffering and heartbreak are no respecters of persons. She represents vast numbers of people today who have searched for comfort, for hope, for peace and have not found it. Some are suffering physically, but some have even greater pain. A person said to me only a few days ago, "Twenty years ago I committed a sin and it has burdened my conscience ever since."

Then the story says, "When she heard of Jesus, came . . . ." Of course, we realize that she had tried everything else and Jesus was her last resort, her last hope. On the other hand, may it be said to her glory that the first time she heard of Him, she came. She had been sick for twelve years. Jesus had only been known for a few months. There were no books at that time about Christ, no newspapers were spreading His fame. There were no churches organized for the purpose of telling the world about Christ. This woman had only heard a rumor about Jesus, yet she acted on that.

How different with so many today. Since childhood, the name of Jesus has been well-known to us. On radio and television, in the newspapers and magazines His name has been spread. The best scholars have written books about Him which are easily available. Throughout the cities, towns and countrysides the spires of churches are reminding us to lift our eyes upward. There are uncounted multitudes whose lives are a testimony of what Christ can do.

Surely all of us can sing, "We have heard the joyful sound, Jesus saves." Yet the tragedy is that though we have heard, we have not come to give Him a chance with us.

HOW SHE TALKED TO HERSELF

In this story of the woman who had been sick for twelve years we read, "For she said, If I may touch but His clothes, I shall be whole." That is a wonderful statement. Look at the first part, "For she said." Matthew points out "she said within herself" (9:21). What we say to other people is important, but what we say to ourselves is far more important. It is good to learn how to speak in public, but it is better to learn how to talk to ourselves.

She might have talked to herself about how she had suffered. Not only was her body racked with pain, but also she had lost the opportunity to be a wife and mother and to have a home. She had suffered repeated disappointments. It would have been so easy to have told herself there was no hope. Her suffering was not her fault and she could have become bitter.

In similar circumstances, some people talk about the injustices of God or the unfairness of men. Some admit their mistakes but excuse themselves with alibis. Some develop self-pity and really reach the point of enjoying their bad circumstances. Sometimes sickness is a convenient escape for us. Many nervous breakdowns, I would say most, are subconsciously desired.

When life is going badly with you, how do you talk to yourself? This woman had heard what Jesus had done for others and she believed. She said, "If I could just touch Him. I won't ask Him to come to my house. I won't ask Him to put His hands on my head. I won't even ask Him to speak to me. If I could just touch Him.

And where should I touch Him? On the head? No, I am not worthy of that. On the hand? No, that would be too familiar. If I could just touch His clothes."

Through the crowd she made her way to Him, but she made no effort to claim His attention or even to let Him see her. She did touch His clothes, but notice where she touched—"the hem of His garment" (Matt. 9:20)—the very lowest part. What a lovely humility we see in her. I've known people who were too proud even to get on their knees to talk to Him. What a complete faith! Some refuse to believe, no matter how many miracles God might perform. But this woman believed there was healing even in the hem of His garment. Of course, she was healed.

No one in the crowd even noticed her. That is, no one but Jesus. He felt the power go out of Him. He knew that somebody's faith had tied into His strength. So He said, "Who touched me?" Impatiently, even sarcastically, the disciples answered, "Thou seest the multitude thronging thee, and sayest thou, Who touched me?"

Luke tells us that Jesus replied, "Somebody hath touched me" (8:46). It has been splendidly pointed out that this woman began as Nobody, but by touching Christ she became Somebody, and in the receiving of His mercy represents Everybody who has faith in Him.

CHRIST FELT THE TOUCH

To the woman who touched His garment and was healed, Jesus said, "Daughter, thy faith hath made thee whole." Look at that woman—all she possessed was faith; her money had all been spent. She was not in some beautiful church. Doubtless she would have been ashamed of her clothes if she had gone to church. She was out on the street on a weekday. She had no private conference with Christ. She was just one of a crowd. Yet the moment she touched even the hem of His garment He felt it, and stopped to find her.

To the disciples it was preposterous that He would notice just one person in the midst of such a crowd. And even today it seems equally preposterous to many that God is concerned about just one person. In another place, Jesus tells about how God clothes the grass of the field and how He provides for the birds of the air. Then Jesus asks if God would do so much for something which will last only a little while, how much more would He do for a human being made in His image and who will last forever. In the light of those facts He rebukes us by saying, "O ye of little faith" (Matt. 6:25-30).

I like the reply of the old colored woman to the census-taker. He asked, "What is the number of your children?" She replied, "They ain't got numbers, they got names." We talk about the number of people there are, but God thinks about our names. "He calleth his own sheep by name," said Jesus (John 10:3).

Don't say, "God is not interested in me." Remember that the human touch can draw on the power of God and claim His attention. The story says, "Jesus looked round about to see her." Her act of faith opened the door to fellowship and friendship with Him.

There are those who feel there is no real power to be received from Christ. We sing, "And He walks with me, and He talks with me, And He tells me I am His own," but for many that is just a song. It is not a real experience. The trouble is that we are out of touch with Him. It is possible to be in the midst of a crowd where Jesus is and yet never touch Him. I see that very thing happen again and again in a church service. We are one of the crowd, we feel our need, we sing, we listen to the sermon, but we go away unhelped. We have come close to Him, but we did not touch Him.

How can you touch Christ? First, you approach Him through the means of prayer. Second, you believe He hears your prayer and answers it. Third, you accept His answer and you do what he says to do. That sounds simple, but that is the way to do it.

When you faithfully do those three things you will immediately feel His power flowing into you. He likely will not speak to you audibly as He did to the woman. But He will speak through your heart and conscience. You will know what He wants you to do and He will know what He should do.

Let the faith you have touch Christ. He will know you have touched Him, even in the midst of a crowd.

9. TAKING THE HANDICAP OUT OF THE MIND

The Miracle of Straightening the Hunchbacked Woman

LUKE 13:11-13

———————

ONE OF THE MOST marvelous stories in the Bible is just three verses long, but it says a lot. "And he was teaching in one of the synagogues on the sabbath. And, behold, there was a woman which had a spirit of infirmity eighteen years, and was bowed together, and could in no wise lift up herself. And when Jesus saw her, he called her to him, and said unto her, Woman, thou art loosed from thine infirmity. And he laid his hands on her: and immediately she was made straight, and glorified God."

Here was a woman who was badly crippled. For eighteen years her back had been bent almost double. No doubt she suffered a great deal of pain in her body. She walked with difficulty. Her housework was an unusually hard burden. Probably she had difficulty sleeping at night. Because of her bent back, she never knew what it was to be really comfortable, either sitting or lying in the bed.

Eighteen years is a long time to be like that; it had become a great mental burden to her. Not only was her body bent, but her spirit had been warped. Notice that Luke points out that she had a "spirit of infirmity." To be handicapped in body is bad, but when that handicap gets into our minds it is far worse.

All the time this woman was conscious of her bent back. Whenever people looked at her, she felt they were thinking of her crippled condition. She painfully realized that she was not pretty and attractive to other people. There was built up in her a sense of inferiority. She would see other women whose bodies were straight and strong and no doubt she felt bitterness and resentment. The "spirit of infirmity" is much harder to overcome than the infirmity itself.

She was "bowed together," bent over. That means that she walked around all the time with her eyes on the ground. To look up was an added effort that she probably did not make often. She saw the dirt and the filth of the world. She missed the blue skies, the birds in the air, the rainbows and the sunsets. Her bent back obscured from her view the beautiful and inspiring things of life. I am sure she had become a miserable, hopeless person. She lost her vision, her dreams, her high purposes.

I have come to know many people with a "spirit of infirmity." They let some handicap or some setback get into their minds and make them bitter and complaining. They lose all incentive for life and they allow themselves to sink into despair and cynicism. They become critical, pessimistic and unhappy.

Their "bent back" may be some physical handicap. Or it may be some great loss like the death of a child. Or it might be seeing some other person pass them in the procession of life and gain a higher place than they have been able to reach. I know a boy who wanted to go to medical school but he did not have the money. Because of his disappointment he is now sour and bitter.

All of us have infirmities of one kind or another. The tragedy occurs when we let that infirmity take possession of our spirits, instead of developing a spirit that takes possession of the infirmity.

"LOOSED FROM THINE INFIRMITY"

May it be said in the woman's favor that she did something to help herself. Many people, under the weight of some infirmity, have given up and quit. Though for eighteen years she had gone about "bowed together," she kept on going. That is good.

One thing she did was go to church. She might have turned her bitterness against God. Some do that. But it never helps to curse the mechanic when our car breaks down. He is the one who can help. And when some circumstance of life weighs heavily upon us, often God is the only one who can help. The Bible says, "She could in no wise lift up herself." It is a marvelous time in our lives when we realize we are not sufficient unto ourselves and look to a higher power. She went to church because she needed the help she could find there.

That day Jesus saw her. Immediately His heart went out to her in compassion. Christ always helps when we give Him a chance. Notice carefully what He did. He said, "Woman, thou art loosed from thine infirmity."

That doesn't mean He straightened her back. He did later on, but that was not necessary. He did something better than straightening her back—He gave her the inner strength to live happily and gloriously in spite of her bent back. He so changed her mental attitude that whether or not her back was bent, from then on it just did not matter.

So often do we recall St. Paul's experience. He had a handicap that troubled him greatly. He prayed earnestly that this "thorn in the flesh" be removed. God could have removed it but God didn't. Instead, He gave him the "grace to bear it." And St. Paul said of it: "Most gladly therefore will I rather glory in my infirmities, that the power of Christ may rest upon me" (II Cor. 12:9). His weakness became his pathway to the strength of Christ in his life. Many times God's power comes into our lives through our hardships, our sorrows and our deepest needs. And we become stronger than we would have been without our need.

We all face circumstances in life that make it hard for us. But in the facing up to those circumstances we gain power. The tragedy is when we allow those circumstances to get inside of us and break our spirits. Dr. Fosdick quoted the prayer of a devout old Negro man. He prayed: "Lord, help me to understand that you ain't gwine to let nothing come my way that you and I can't handle together." That faith takes the dread and fear out of living and gives us a confident assurance.

General William Booth, founder of the Salvation Army, when informed that he was going blind said, "I have done what I could for God and people with two eyes. Now I will do what I can for God and people without eyes." That is the courage that God gives to those who trust Him.

THE BRACES REMOVED FROM THE MIND

Some time ago I was speaking for a few days in a college. In the afternoons I would talk privately with any of the students who wanted to see me. One of the ones who came was the most attractive girl on the campus. She was beautiful and sweet but wore braces on her legs and could hardly walk. She told me she was voted the happiest girl on campus. But she said they just didn't know. In truth, she was the unhappiest girl there.

As she watched other girls play tennis, run upstairs, go to dances, she felt bitterness deep down. She kept up a front but she told me that night after night she cried herself to sleep. I said, "Let me tell you a story."

It was about a very prominent newspaper editor. When he was a boy he had polio which left him with braces on his legs. As he grew older he realized he could not run or climb trees like other boys. Little by little he began to feel he could not keep up in the race of life or climb the ladder of success like others could. What was happening to him was that those braces on his legs were getting into his mind.

His father had told him that some day he would carry him to the big church in the city and there he would be healed. Finally the day came. As he walked down the aisle his braces went "thump, thump, thump." The people looking his way made him feel very self-conscious. They knelt at the altar and very earnestly his father prayed. After a while the father turned to the boy and said, "Son, I have the answer. You have been healed."

They got up and started back up the aisle. But his braces were still going "thump, thump, thump." He could not tell any difference, but before they got out of the church a feeling came over him that he was all right; that in spite of the braces he could be a successful man. From that moment on he never worried again about those braces and he went on to a very successful career. What happened was that though God left the braces on his legs, He took them out of his mind. Jesus did for him what He did for the woman whose back had been bent for eighteen years. He said to her, "Thou art loosed from thine infirmity."

Helen Keller was blind, deaf and dumb, but she said, "I thank God for my handicaps, for through them I have found myself, my work and my God."

Evelyn Harrala was born with neither hands nor feet, yet she became a musician in great demand over the country. Victor Hugo was banished into exile, yet instead of being bitter over it he used the time to write *Les Miserables,* one of the finest novels ever written.

Robert Louis Stevenson suffered all the time, yet in the midst of his suffering he wrote stories that will never die. Millet, the French painter, was so poor that he and his wife were both cold and hungry; yet in those circumstances he painted some of the most soul-satisfying pictures to be found anywhere.

All of us are handicapped in some way. But there is never a situation that God's power cannot make us able to overcome. And by going on to victory over our circumstances and ourselves, we reach the place attained by the woman whose bent back Jesus healed. She ended up by "glorifying God." She found joy through victory in Christ.

10. THE POWER TO ACT ON OUR DREAMS

*The Miracle of Healing the Man
with the Withered Hand*

MARK 3:1-5

THERE IS A STORY which begins: "And he entered again into the synagogue; and there was a man there which had a withered hand." There was a man who was severely handicapped. He could think of a lot of things he wanted to do, but his hand was withered. He could not translate his thoughts into deeds. The hand represents action and his hand was withered.

In my work as a minister I have met a lot of people with this very handicap. They dream and they plan, but somehow they never quite have what it takes actually to carry out those dreams. A man was telling me recently that for years he was wanted to become active in the work of the church and make his life count for more. But somehow he has kept putting it off. He can't quite take the step. He has the right idea, but his hand is withered.

I have talked with many people who have a liquor problem. But I have never talked with any who weren't quick to say it was hurting their lives and they were going to give it up. But so often their hands are withered. They can't quite carry out their good thoughts. They lack the power to translate their desires into actions.

A man told me he was thinking of becoming a tither. I asked him how long he had been thinking about it and he said for several years. He wants to tithe but his hand is withered. He doesn't have the power actually to do what he really wants to do.

In fact, to some extent we all are afflicted with this handicap of the withered hand. We have so many good things in mind that we never put into deeds. The other day I was at a funeral and a friend was telling me how long he had known this man who had died. He told me that when he heard his friend was sick he intended to visit him, but he just kept putting it off. And now the man had died and it was too late.

There is an old saying, "If wishes were horses, all beggars would ride." It is good to dream of the fine things we want to do and be. Before Lindbergh flew the Atlantic, he dreamed about it. Edison thought about the electric light. All great actions begin in our minds, but the failures are those who never act on their dreams.

Look into your own mind and see how many good things you have there which you have thought about doing. But as yet you haven't had the right opportunity, or you lack the ability, or you don't have enough training, and haven't had time, or you don't feel like it—all those excuses are just other names for your handicap of a withered hand. You think well but you don't act.

To the man with the withered hand Jesus said, "Stand forth." That is, you have drifted long enough. Now let's face up to the situation. There comes a time when we must take command of our thoughts.

WILL POWER AND WON'T POWER

Oliver Wendell Holmes said, "Many people die with their music still in them." To some extent that is true of all of us. We have the abilities to do many things that we never actually do. Emerson said, "You never know what you can do until you try." And right at this point we need the power of religious faith. Under the inspiration of Christ we accomplish things we never before dared try to do.

When Jesus met in church that day a man with a withered hand, he first told him to "Stand forth." He wanted the man's full attention. Then Christ said, "Stretch forth thine hand." Jesus did not talk about how bad it is to have a withered hand. He did not ask how long the man's hand had been withered. He did not ask why it was withered. He just said, "Stretch forth thine hand." In other words, we've passed the time for talk and come to the time for action.

But the man was incapable of action by himself. Many times he had wanted to use that hand but he couldn't. His will power was not strong enough to overcome the weakness of his body. So often we make resolutions but we fail to keep them. We fail because there is an opposing force within us that overcomes our will.

An old colored man was trying to get a balky mule to move, but without success. Somebody said, "Uncle, why don't you try your will power on that mule?" He replied, "I done tried it but it don't do no good. He's using his won't power."

Within each of us there is both a will power and a won't power. We have high desires but at the same time we tell ourselves that it's no use to try. We say, "I will" but our minds shout back at us, "You can't—you won't." "Won't power" is simply will power in reverse. And it is easier for most of us to drift backward than to push forward. So, in our own strength we fail.

We remind ourselves of Moses. As a young man he bitterly resented the fact that his people were in slavery. In anger one day he even killed one of the Egyptians. No doubt he felt he must do something to free his people but then he realized the hopelessness of the task. He thought about freedom but his hand was withered—incapable of action.

He went off into the country, and day after day as he watched over the sheep he had time to think, but think is all he did. Probably some day he intended to do something, but the time slipped by. The weeks went into months and finally forty years had gone by. Then God decided He would take a hand.

First, He got Moses' attention. To get it, He sent a bush on fire but never let it burn up. God may do many things to get our attention. Sometimes He may even put us on our backs to give us a chance to look up. With Moses' attention God spoke, telling him to go lead his people out. But Moses made excuses. God said, "I'll give you the power." And with the help of God Moses became mightier than Pharaoh's army, and stronger even than the Red Sea.

YOU CAN DO IT

To the man whose hand was withered Jesus said, "Stretch forth thine hand." Notice the complete confidence of Christ. He has no doubt the man could and would respond. Jesus is saying, "You can do it." Up to now the man had not been able to do it. His own will power was insufficient. But now the will of Christ became his will and he could then do things he couldn't do before.

I see this very thing happen often in church. At the close of every Sunday night service I invite the people to pray on their knees at the altar. In that service many, many lives have been changed. What is the secret? There, in the presence of God and with the support of other praying people, our minds are opened to His mind and our wills are surrendered to His will and our hearts receive His power. I could write a book about the experiences I know people have had at the altar. Let me give just one:

A man called me the other day and said, "I've quit my job." I knew something of his circumstances and I knew he was having a hard time. He was in debt and my first thought was he had just given up in despair. I asked him to tell me all about it. He told me that for ten years he had been unhappy in his work and that he was not making any progress. Time and again he had thought of trying to better himself but he just couldn't quite get up the nerve to try.

Then one night he prayed at the altar and he seemed to hear the Lord saying, "Go ahead, with my help you can do it." For the first time in several years he felt relieved and relaxed. In his calm state of mind he could think clearer. He thought of a man who might help him and he resolved to go see that man the next morning. As he drove into the parking lot the next morning, that very man drove in right behind him. He said to him, "I would like to talk with you."

Together they walked on up to that man's office and my friend told him of his decision to do something else. The man knew of no opportunities right then but promised to look around and phone him when he found something. Before lunch that day the man did phone. One of the partners in a business had died and the other partner was looking for someone to buy that interest.

My friend went to see him but said he didn't have any money. The other man worked out a plan by which he could pay his share out of the profits of the business and it was fixed up that way. Then my friend told me he wondered why the Lord didn't do it for him ten years ago. I said, "You were not willing to listen to God until you got desperate. Then you opened your heart to God and you became willing to do something."

Many times we hear a voice saying, "Stretch forth thine hand." But we hold back, we hesitate, we make excuses. We are planning to do the right thing—sometime. We are going to turn from our weak ways—sometime. But as long as we trust our own strength, we will never do it. Our hands are withered—His power can make us what we ought to be.

11. YOUR DISTURBED MIND MAY BE OF GOD

The Miracle of Healing the Man with an Unclean Spirit

MARK 5:1-20

ONE DAY there came to Jesus a man who was possessed by an "unclean spirit" or "demon." Throughout the New Testament we find references to demons and unclean spirits, but we have a tendency to regard those stories as mere ancient superstitions. However, as we study those stories of demon-possessed people, we find that they describe actual human situations that we frequently see today.

The actions of the people today are the same as they were in Jesus' day. The only difference is that modern psychology and psychiatry have coined a lot of new names like paranoia, schizophrenia, and the like. Today we talk about mental delusions and split personalities. In New Testament times they simply said a demon had moved into the person and taken possession.

This man who came to Jesus said: "My name is Legion: for we are many." We can understand that because we ourselves often feel that we are more than one person. There is the person in us who aspires to high and holy living. But there are other persons which seem to take possession of us. I have had people say to me, in explaining some action, "I was not myself." We become possessed by some passion such as hate, fear, lust, greed, selfishness, and under the power of those spirits we do and say things foreign to our real selves.

Even St. Paul had this experience. He said, "For the good that I would, I do not: but the evil which I would not, that I do" (Romans 7:19). That is, at times he did not do what he really wanted to do and he did do some things which he did not want to do. It was as if there was in him a demon or foreign spirit which sometimes got the upper hand and controlled him against his will. Our modern studies have helped us better to understand and treat mental disturbances of various types, but the people are still the same today as in Bible times. To some extent, every person is demon-possessed. That is, we possess some tendency to act against the highest and best within us. And when that tendency gets out of control we become unbalanced or even insane.

The man in Jesus' story lived in the graveyard. A lot of people today have moved into the graveyards. Their physical bodies are still alive but their dreams and hopes are dead. They have no high purpose to live for and no real reason for existence. They do not thrill to the dawning of a new day; instead, life is just a treadmill on which to trudge laboriously without ever getting anywhere.

For some people, all the good was yesterday. They have no desire for new adventures and discoveries. The word progress has no meaning for them. They have given up and quit. People become possessed by such demons as past defeats, disappointments, feelings of inadequacy or inferiority and the like. They really stop living and move into some mental graveyard slowly to die.

WHEN CHRIST DISTURBS

Life is so constituted that no person can stand still. Either we are progressing or we are dying. Either we are getting better or we are getting worse. Either we are helping ourselves or we are hurting ourselves. The demon-possessed man who came to Jesus had moved into the graveyard. But even there he could not remain in a neutral state. Not doing himself good, he began hurting himself. The Bible says that night and day he was "cutting himself with stones."

Into my study have come many people who, because of some uncontrolled appetite, temper, harmful habit, selfish desire, hate or envy, or some other "evil spirit," are making wrecks of themselves. We are possessed by things that we know are hurting us, yet somehow we can't set ourselves free.

The man who had come to Jesus had become physically dangerous and the only solution the people had was to bind him with "fetters and chains," that is to meet force with force. We boast of our great progress, yet sometimes we wonder. The world seems possessed by a spirit of war. To meet it we pile up more and more super-bombs. Someone says something evil about us and we say something worse in return. We have not yet learned that conquering evil with great evil is never a solution.

Watch Jesus as He deals with this man. To begin with he begs the Lord, "torment me not." But Jesus frequently is a tormenter of people. There are times when Christ comes as the comforter, other times as a disturber. Sometimes He brings peace, sometimes a sword. He may be a gentle breeze which soothes our wounded spirit, or He may be a violent storm which severely shakes us. We see Him weeping at the grave of a friend and we also see Him with a whip in His hand, driving people before Him.

I have a friend whose broken arm had not been set straight. Not only was his arm crooked but it was also very painful. The specialist might have soothed and comforted him. Instead, he took an instrument and broke the arm again. That might have seemed cruel but it was necessary in order to reset the arm straight.

And sometimes Christ upsets and disturbs us. He may throw us into circumstances which will change our way of living. It may be that just when it seems we have everything fixed, it all becomes unfixed. That business or friend on which we have come to lean so heavily may be taken away and we become forced to learn again how to walk by ourselves.

Life itself is a disturbing influence. Styles change and we are forced to change with them. New knowledge is constantly being brought forth and we must either keep up or be laid on the shelf. Living in a world like this it is impossible just to settle down. The procession will leave us behind.

The other night a man phoned me to say, "I am so miserable I can't stand it. I have done wrong and I must get it straightened out." Thank God that He disturbs us. If you feel agitated and disturbed, it may be because God is working with you.

The one thing we want is peace and contentment. But sometimes God will not let us be content in the state we are in. Because He wants the best for us, He will disturb and agitate us to keep us from being satisfied in some unsatisfactory life. Just as the physician may break a crooked bone in order to set it straight, God may break a wrong spirit in order to give us a chance to possess the right spirit.

By my bedside I keep an alarm clock. I don't like alarm clocks. There is no more distasteful sound to me than a clock alarming. It disturbs my sleep and though I dislike being disturbed, I set the clock. Why? Because each day I have new work to do. I have new opportunities to possess. And unless I am disturbed I will sleep my chances away.

Sometimes Christ is the divine alarmer. He disturbs our conscience because He has a better way for us to live. He makes us dissatisfied with the good because He wants us to have the best. He makes us ashamed of our ignorance because He wants us to learn. He shakes us out of our complacency because He has new mountains for us to climb which offer wider horizons.

So when a mentally disturbed man came to Christ, Christ disturbed him still more. At first the man resented it. He begged Christ to let him alone. Someone has well pointed out that God is one of three things to us. At first He is merely a void. Our belief in God is vague and unreal. But sometimes we are thrown into circumstances which our resources are insufficient to meet. We become forced to face God and often He then becomes our enemy. He makes demands which we find painful to meet. He demands new discipline and changes in our ways. We resent His interferences. But as we respond to God He becomes our friend. Void—enemy—friend. God is one of those three to us.

To this man possessed by wrong spirit Christ said, "What is thy name?" If you miss the significance of that, you miss the whole story. In Bible times a person was given a name which described the person. To know his name was to know the person. Furthermore, to know the person was to have power over him. Read Genesis 32. There you have Jacob wrestling with the angel. Jacob told the angel his name but the angel would not tell Jacob his name. The angel had power over Jacob, but Jacob had no power over the angel.

When Jesus asked the man his name, He was saying:

"Trust me. Put yourself · in my hands. Let me have power over you." The man told Christ his name. He was willing to confide in Christ, to put before Christ his life. We may call it confession or opening our hearts to God. And the very moment the man put himself in the hands of Christ, the evil which dwelt within him lost its power and was driven out.

We say, "I will do better," but we don't live up to it. The evil within us is stronger than we are. But when by faith we seek God's help we have a source of strength sufficient to overcome the evil and set us free.

Finally, Luke tells us they found the man "clothed, and in his right mind." His way of life became "sensible." He began to live according to the principles of wisdom and truth. And into such a life Christ leads all who commit their ways unto His way.

12. WHY DO WE SUFFER?

*The Miracle of Healing the
Man Born Blind*

JOHN 9:1-41

THE OTHER DAY I visited a dear lady suffering intense pain as a result of cancer. She was so weak that I had to bend low to hear her ask in a whisper, "Is God now punishing me for something I have done?" At the cemetery just a few weeks ago a young father said to me, "God has taken my little boy because of my sins."

We hear that sort of thing over and over in the presence of pain and sorrow. So we are not surprised to hear the disciples of Christ asking Him about a man suffering from blindness, "Who did sin, this man or his parents, that he was born blind?" The very oldest problem of man is "Why do we suffer?" and the most often accepted answer is that suffering is the price God makes us pay for our sins.

The oldest book in the Bible is Job. There we have a record of a man losing his wealth, his children and his health. Though Job had lived what seemed to be a good life, his friends believed that the fact of his trials and troubles proved that he had done wrong. They said, "Whoever perished, being innocent?" (Job 4:7).

Long before Jesus' day the people had been taught that everything that happens is a direct act of God. They believed that the storms, earthquakes, defeat in war, sickness in body all came at God's command. To believe that anything could happen which God did not command would be to lessen His power, they felt. On the other hand, if God is good, why would He cause His children to suffer? The only explanation they could make was to place the blame on man. Man sins and that causes his punishment, they reasoned.

If you saw a father punishing his child, you would reason that either the father is mean and delights in seeing his child suffer, or that the child has done wrong and that a reasonable punishment is the obligation of the father. So, in the presence of the blind man's suffering, the disciples did not doubt that it was God's affliction because of sin. Their only question was in regard to who sinned, the man or his parents.

Jesus did not accept that theory for a moment. Quickly He said, "Neither hath this man sinned, nor his parents." He did not give the reason for the man's suffering but He does emphatically say it was not caused by sin. We do know that all sin eventually causes suffering. But it does not follow that all suffering is caused by sin. Jesus made that clear.

Jesus might have taken that occasion to give a sermon on the causes and explanations of suffering. But He does not do it. Instead, He said, "The works of God should be made manifest in him." That is, here is a man in need, let us not argue about the causes. Better to give ourselves to the work of God which is helping those who need help.

HE DOES SOMETHING ABOUT IT

Instead of talking about why a man was blind, Jesus set about to help him. That was the theme of His life. Mark tells us "He went about doing good." Some people are so busy explaining things that they do not have time to do much. I doubt if Jesus attended many forums or discussion groups. He was so busy changing people and situations that He had little time for idle talk and speculations.

He might have preached lengthy sermons on the dignity of labor, temptation, how to enjoy life, the immortality of the soul, the worth of children and the fact that God answers prayer. Instead, He worked in a carpenter's shop, He met and conquered temptation in the wilderness, He went to parties and laughed with other happy people, He raised the dead, He stopped His sermon to love little children, and after He prayed "the power of the Lord was present."

He might have talked long and loud about the need of man for human sympathy, the worth of womanhood, the blessing of humility and the equal worth of all men. Instead, He wept at the grave of a friend, He treated all women with deep respect, He took a towel and washed His disciples' feet, He gave His time to the poor and outcasts.

Instead of talking about how He could transform lives, He took a harlot and made her the first herald of His resurrection. Instead of arguing that spirit is stronger than matter, He walked on the water. Instead of preaching that people need bread, He fed the multitude. Instead of telling how bad it is to be crippled, He said, "Arise, take up thy bed, and walk." Instead of merely telling people they should forgive, while He was dying and being spit upon He prayed, "Father, forgive them." Instead of theorizing about God, He said, "I am the way."

So we do not expect Him to take time to argue the problem of pain and suffering. In the presence of need His concern is to do something about it.

There is a legend that a man was caught in a bed of quicksand. Confucius saw him and remarked, "There is evidence men should stay out of such places." Buddha came by and said, "Let that life be a lesson to the rest of the world." Mohammed said about the man, "Alas, it is the will of Allah." The Hindu said to him, "Cheer up friend, you will return to earth in another form." But when Jesus saw him He said, "Give me your hand, brother, and I will pull you out."

If we come to Him to argue and speculate about the sins and needs of our lives, we will go away disappointed. But when we come to Him with a need, and want—really want—something done about it, it will be done. The Bible tells us, "For God sent not his Son into the world to condemn the world; but that the world through him might be saved" (John 3:17). Some people are so busy condemning sin that they have no time to do anything about it. Jesus was so busy saving the sinner that He had no time or reason to condemn.

So whatever our need, if we want help we can find it in Him.

FAITH AND OBEDIENCE

To heal the man born blind Jesus "spat on the ground, and made clay of the spittle, and he anointed the eyes of the blind man with the clay, and said unto him, Go, wash in the pool of Siloam."

On another occasion Jesus healed a blind man instantly and with a mere word (Mark 10:46-52). In another case, He healed a blind man in stages, or by a process (Mark 8:22-26). Likewise He works His miracles in people today. Sometimes He does what we ask immediately. Sometimes He does it over a period of time. Sometimes He must prepare us further for the receiving of His power.

The putting of the clay on the man's eyes was for a definite purpose. The people in that day believed that the saliva of a good man contained healing power. When Jesus put His saliva on the man's eyes it was for the purpose of arousing faith and hope in the man. As you study His miracles, you learn that He required faith. This man had no faith so Christ must help him to create it.

He then sent the man to wash in the pool of Siloam. Why did He do that? Because He wanted to teach the man obedience.

Here we see clearly the two steps Christ requires—faith and obedience. Those are the steps to find the solution to any problem. Take cancer, for example. First we must believe the answer to it can be found. This belief will cause scientists to give their time and talents in long and tedious research. It will cause the public to make possible that research through the support that is necessary.

It was believed possible to create those powerful new bombs we have. Therefore, scientists went to work on it and the government put many millions into plant facilities and other resources. Do we doubt that we could find the answer to cancer with the same amount of research and resources? We can eliminate cancer whenever we really want to.

The scientist first believes. Then he faithfully follows the truth as he discovers it through research.

When we believe there is a solution to any problem and faithfully take each step God reveals to us, eventually we will find the answer. It may not be the answer we thought we should find but it will be the right answer. If we want the power of Christ, we must trust and obey.

Pierre and Marie Curie had made 487 experiments to try to separate radium from pitchblend. All had failed. Finally Pierre Curie said, "It can't be done; it can't be done. Maybe in a hundred years it can be done, but never in our lifetime." Madame Curie replied: "If it takes a hundred years it will be a pity, but I dare not do less than work for it so long as I have life." There is faith and obedience.

The blind man was healed. It came through the power of Christ and his own faith and obedience. Whatever our need, He stands ready and able whenever we take the two necessary steps.

13. THE STEPS OF DIVINE HEALING IN SLOW MOTION

The Miracle of Healing the Afflicted Boy

MARK 9:1-29

———

ONE OF THE major activities of Christ was healing the sick. In fact, two-thirds of all His reported acts were acts of healing. As we study His miracles we realize that

He did something above and beyond our psychological techniques and understanding. His miracles are on a level far above psychology. He possessed spiritual power.

In the ninth chapter of Mark, we have laid before us step by step the method He used. Most of His miracles happened so quickly we cannot analyze them. To the crippled He merely said, "Take up thy bed and walk." To the winds and waves He said, "Peace, be still," and it was done. One woman just touched the hem of His garment and she was healed. But in Mark 9 we have the process in slow motion so we can see it.

It begins with the transfiguration experience on the mountain. "After six days Jesus taketh with him Peter, and James, and John, and leadeth them up into a high mountain apart by themselves" (Mark 9:2). Let's look at three important steps there.

(1) "After six days." Six days in the Bible is the symbol for honest work. God finished the Creation in six days. In the Ten Commandments we are told, "Six days shalt thou labor" (Ex. 20:9). Work is a part of the business of living and we cannot enter the presence of God on lazy feet. Prayer is never a substitute for work. The "mountain top" experiences, the spiritual heights, are gained partly as a result of work.

(2) "Jesus taketh with him Peter, and James, and John." There are two comments to make about that. First, those were the three closest to Him and between them there was a deep friendship. Praying alone is powerful but praying with those whose spirits are harmonious with ours is even more powerful. We remember that Jesus said, "Where two or three are gathered together in my name, there am I in the midst of them" (Matt. 18:20). We gain support from each other. In a church service where we join with a large number of other people who have faith and believe in prayer, we are likely

to possess more completely the Spirit of God. I often suggest to people who have a particular prayer that they get one or more prayer-partners. I myself have been a partner in prayer with many and have seen marvelous results from it.

Second, in his *Paradiso,* Dante says that Peter represents faith; James, hope; and John, love. Whether there is actual Scriptural basis for that or not, the fact is that those qualities are the essential ingredients of prayer: faith that the answer is possible; hope that causes us to concentrate on the solutions rather than on the problems; love that rids our lives of selfishness, of jealousy and envy, that teaches us the meaning of sacrificial living.

(3) On the mountain they had a tremendous spiritual experience. Later Jesus was to demonstrate His miracle-working power in the healing of a little boy at the foot of that mountain, but first He received the power Himself. We cannot expect to be able to use God's power when we ourselves have not experienced it.

There we see the preparation for the miracle which followed.

CHRIST CAME "DOWNHILL"

After the great transfiguration experience of Christ and some of His disciples on the mountain, we read, "they came down from the mountain." In that sentence we have the key to all of Christ's miracles. Simon Peter was so thrilled by the spiritual experience on the mountain that he wanted just to stay there. But Christ could see the entire experience. The receiving of the spiritual power was only one side. The expression of that power was the other side. Before any experience is complete it must have expression.

Many people seek the beauty and inspiration of religious faith but so often they fail to relate it to the tragic need and suffering about them. When we say a person is "going downhill" we think of it in a bad sense. But from every mountain-top spiritual experience, Christ always came "downhill." As Sidney Lanier expressed it in "The Song of the Chattahoochee" (Charles Scribner's Sons, New York):

Downward the voices of Duty call—
Downward, to toil and be mixed with the main,
The dry fields burn, and the mills are to turn,
And a myriad flowers mortally yearn,

Christ ascended the mountain of prayer; He came down into the valley of service.

At the foot of the mountain Jesus found a father who had come, bringing his little boy who was afflicted with epilepsy. Notice carefully the three steps of the miracle of healing. First, the concern of Christ. To the father He said, "How long is it ago since this came unto him?" He wanted to know; He was willing to listen to the problem. This is an important part of the practice of psychiatry.

Once a woman came to Dr. Freud suffering from a seemingly incurable disease. He told her that it was useless to come to him but she begged him to see her and listen to her tell about her trouble. He consented to see her regularly and to his amazement he discovered that she was actually getting well. There is tremendous healing power in having somebody to listen who cares and understands. Therein lies part, only part but an important part, of the value of prayer. God hears us when we pray.

Second, the creation of faith. Jesus said, "If thou canst believe, all things are possible to him that believeth." Notice the word "if" as Jesus used it. It does not apply to His power. A physician might say, "I will heal you if I can." But with Christ there was no question as to His ability. The "if" applied to the other person. God's power is limited only by our faith. "If thou canst believe," He says to you and to me.

Then we read: "The father cried out, and said with tears." Those tears are precious. A man was in to see me about a serious situation in his life and as he talked, tears overflowed his eyes and rolled down his cheeks. As he wiped them away he said, "I know you hate to see a grown man cry." I told him there are times when tears are the highest mark of manhood. The person who never feels deeply enough to cry is a person to be pitied.

No real father can see his afflicted son except with a broken heart. And until we feel our prayers with our hearts as well as our minds, they are not real. We cannot approach God on flippant feet. Prayer is not for triflers.

YOUR FAITH NEED NOT BE COMPLETE

In the story of Christ healing the afflicted boy, the father said: "Lord, I believe; help thou mine unbelief." He was saying he wanted to believe and did, yet his belief was not complete. There was still some doubt in his mind. It is not difficult to understand that father's situation.

Since his boy was a little fellow he had been afflicted, and no one knows how the father must have suffered over it. The realization that his son could not live a normal life was a heavy burden to bear. Surely that father had prayed again and again but up to now had seen no results. No doubt he had carried him to church and had others pray, but still with no results.

Probably the father was a poor man, yet I am sure he

made many sacrifices to have his boy treated by the best doctors. Whenever a new medicine that might help came on the market, the father would buy it. But every effort he made ended in disappointment. Now he had brought his son to Christ. The very fact of his coming was an indication of faith. Surely he wanted to believe, yet he could not help but have some doubt.

The father was not cynical. Even though he had not received the answer to his prayers, he had not turned his back on God. He had not given up and quit trying. He was honest with Christ. He expressed and acted upon the faith he had, but he did not try to hide his doubt. No person believes perfectly. In every human mind there is a mixture of faith and doubt. But the important thing is whether we let ourselves be controlled by the faith we have or by our doubts. We must remember: the miracles come not because we have a perfect faith, but rather because of our faith in a perfect Christ.

In spite of the father's doubts, but because of his faith, Christ did heal the boy. Exactly how He healed I cannot explain. It is a miracle. But we may be sure that the same power, the power of God, is still present and available to every person today, if he will only seek it.

In Matthew's account of this miracle he records Christ as saying, "For verily I say unto you, If ye have faith as a grain of mustard seed, ye shall say unto this mountain, Remove hence to yonder place; and it shall remove; and nothing shall be impossible unto you" (Matt. 17:20). That is, take what faith you have, even if it is as small as a mustard seed, use it and you will find it sufficient for whatever mountain of difficulty there may be in your life.

Finally the disciples, who had tried to heal the boy but had failed, asked Jesus why they could not work the miracle. He replied, "This kind can come forth by nothing, but by prayer and fasting." Prayer is the process of filling your life with God and the consecration of yourself to God's will and purpose. Fasting represents an empty process. It means the ridding of your life of wrong, the forsaking of those things and attitudes which are contrary to the Spirit of God, the taking of self out of the picture and making God first. That is the price we must pay to gain the transforming power of God.

14. WHY DIDN'T CHRIST CONDEMN AN ADULTERESS?

The Miracle of the Woman Taken in Adultery

JOHN 8:1-11

EARLY ONE morning Jesus was in the temple courtyard teaching a group of friends. Suddenly a crowd of men— really a mob—came pushing through. Their faces were set, harsh and stern. In their midst was a woman. We do not know her name. She may have been a common woman of the streets or she may have been one of the respected women of the community.

Perhaps she struggled to free herself. She would have liked to run as far away as possible. Maybe she cried out because of the pain of a strong man's grip on her arm. She was fearfully embarrassed. Her accusers had already made up their minds to stone her to death and since women were stoned without any clothes on, it is likely hers had already been ripped off.

To Jesus they began to pour out their accusations against her. In voices loud enough for everybody to hear they shouted the facts of her shame. She had been caught in adultery. A mob of hardened self-righteous people can be coarse and cruel. They asked Jesus whether or not she could be stoned. It was a cheap trick to trap Him.

If Jesus said not to stone her, He would be repudiating the law of Moses. If He permitted the stoning, He would be going against the law of Rome. If He said to let her go, He would be condoning a sin. If He condemned her, He would not be the merciful Christ the multitudes believed Him to be. The angry mob shouted, "Shall we stone her?"

The Master gave no immediate answer. Instead He turned and began writing on the ground. I think that is one of the loveliest scenes of His life. He was always the perfect gentleman. He knew the woman's embarrassment and He refused to add to it by looking at her. Some people seem to enjoy another's shame, but not Jesus. He would not add to her humiliation and mental agony.

The mob insisted—"Shall we stone her?" The story says, "He lifted himself up." I am sure He took not one backward step. He had no hesitation in looking this mob straight in the eye. Strong and tall He stood before them. He was tender and loving and kind. But He wasn't weak, He was never afraid. With His eyes unwavering and with steel in His voice He said, "He that is without sin among you, let him first cast a stone at her."

Then He stooped down again and began to write on the ground. I wonder what He wrote? There is a legend that He knew those men. They had howled for judgment against this woman, now He began to let judgment descend upon their own heads. He wrote "liar" and looked at a certain man. That man's face turned white, the rock slipped out of his hand, he slunk away.

Murderer, thief, adulterer, drunkard—one by one the penetrating eyes of Christ gazed upon those men. Their stones thudded against the pavement. They hurriedly left until finally Jesus was alone with the accused woman.

ONLY GOD CAN JUDGE

When Jesus said, "He that is without sin among you, let him first cast a stone at her," He was saying both to them and to us that only God has the right to judge. Because of our own sins our judgments are biased. Because of our limited knowledge and understanding of another's heart we do not know all the facts. No less than the righteousness and the knowledge of God is sufficient for judgment and even He waits until the end of our earthly life.

How we so-called Christians need to learn this lesson! We should be ashamed of gossip. I pray that the people of my church might love one another with mercy —forgiving mercy. Pride, bad temper, selfishness, vanity—there are so many sins. None of us have the right to point the accusing finger at another. As we come to church, let us stand by the side of the publican and pray, "God be merciful to me a sinner" (Luke 18:13).

One recently said to me, "I am ashamed to pray after what I have done." I read to that one the story of Christ and the fallen woman. The crowd of accusers were now gone. Those two were now together—alone. What did He say? Did He tell her how terrible her sin was? Did He talk about Hell? Did He shout at her? I am sure His voice was soft and kind. He didn't mention her sin. He said not one word about punishment.

He said, "Woman." That is the same word He used to address His own mother just before He died. Don't miss the significance of that. For this soiled, accused person, our Lord had the same respect that He had for His own mother—the purest of all women of all time. Of course He was saddened because of her wrong, but she was still the child of His Father. In spite of our sins, He loved her and you and me so much that He was willing to give His all—even His life—to save us. Why should anyone hesitate to talk to Him?

"Woman, where are those thine accusers? hath no man condemned thee?" She said, "No man, Lord." Those are the only words the woman spoke. She blamed nobody else. She had no excuse for her conduct. She did not attempt to justify herself. She did not say she was no worse than a lot of other people.

A few moments before His words had the power to drive out a mob of self-righteous accusers. They could not stand within the withering gaze of the Son of God. Now He was looking at this woman—not on her body, but into her heart. From Him a spiritual energy was being discharged into her very soul. She accepted and received Him. The wrong within her could not face the Christ. It was driven out. His will became her will. Repentance, the desire to change, took possession of her.

Jesus then was able to say, "Neither do I condemn thee: go, and sin no more."

SOMETHING BETTER THAN CONDEMNATION

Why didn't Jesus condemn an adulteress? Does it mean that He condones this sin or any other sin? No person who ever comes to know the pure, sinless Christ would say that He condones our sins. He hated sin as He hated hell. Sin is against Him and everything He stood for. Sin was the one thing He warred against. It was sin that crucified Him.

There are two reasons why He didn't condemn the woman. First, it wasn't necessary. Others had already condemned her. Her own conscience had condemned her. The law of Moses, which is the law of God, had condemned her. The one who transgresses God's way is condemned—let us make no mistake about that.

Second, Jesus had something far better to offer than condemnation. "For God sent not his son into the world to condemn the world; but that the world through him might be saved" (John 3:17). Instead of condemnation, He gave her forgiveness. I say gave—she didn't earn it. She couldn't earn it. How could she turn back the pages of her life and wipe away the stains? What had been done had been done.

And let us be slow to become self-righteous in the presence of this fallen woman. Not only are there sins of the body—there are sins of the heart, sins of the mind, sins of the disposition. We are all sinners. We have all come short of His glory. Under the power of His presence, this woman had come to hate her sin and to want to live above it.

I am sure the understanding Christ turned and found a cloak and handed it to her to wear. Now she could walk back through the street without embarrassment. Forgiveness is the cloak for our naked, sinful souls. The Psalmist sings, "Blessed is he whose transgression is forgiven, whose sin is covered" (Ps. 32:1). When God forgives it means that He forgets. Our sin is remembered against us no more.

Surely this woman would not have insulted the Lord by refusing to accept His forgiveness. It would have been ingratitude on her part to have nursed her sense of guilt, to have refused to leave her past behind. In the presence of Christ she had been accused, she had been convicted, she had been judged—but she had not been condemned. She had been forgiven!

I can see her as she rose from the ground. She stood at her full height. Her head was held up. There was a smile on her face, a spring in her step, a joy in her heart. We do not know her name nor her circumstances in life. But of one thing we can be sure, she was never the same person again.

The Son of God healed the sick, caused the blind to see, quieted the winds and the waves. But in this woman, defeated and condemned by sin, He worked the greatest miracle of all.

> He breaks the power of canceled sin,
> He sets the pris'ner free;
> His blood can make the foulest clean;
> His blood availed for me.

He did it for her—He will do it for any one of us who will accept it.

15. DOES GOD EVER SEND THE STORM?

The Miracle of Walking on the Water

MATTHEW 14:22-23

ONE OF THE most appealing stories in all the Bible is the one about Jesus walking on the water. "And straightway Jesus constrained [made] his disciples to get into a ship." There was good reason for sending the disciples away. Jesus had just fed the five thousand and, as a result, they wanted to make Him king. We like to enthrone those who will give us something.

Jesus had come to establish a kingdom, but He was not a cheap politician willing to bribe people with a crust of bread. His kingdom must be established by making men fit to live in it. He knew that mere outward prosperity without inward change would never be a permanent society. The multitude always wants to make a king out of those who furnish easy bread. But Jesus came not to make life easy but to make men good.

Jesus' disciples were about to be swept along with the thinking of the crowd. So to give them a chance to regain their balance, the Lord made His disciples get in a boat and go off by themselves. Then we read, "He sent the multitudes away." We like to go where the crowds are. We like to let the crowd control our thinking. Individual responsibility is always a burden to bear. To shift the load to the crowd is so much easier. "Everybody else is doing it, so why should I worry about it?" we say.

Also, we like the approval of the crowd. But there come times when it is necessary to forget the crowd and what is popular and instead to think of God and what His will is. So Jesus went out into the mountain alone to pray.

William Penn in his *Fruits of Solitude,* wrote: "Till we are persuaded to stop and step aside out of the prospect of things, it will be impossible to make a right adjustment of ourselves . . . The wise man is he who from time to time withdraws from the crowd and looks at it from the standpoint of the eternal." When Père Didon was exiled to Corsica, Pasteur wrote him: "You will come back with your soul still loftier, your thoughts more firm, more disengaged from earthly things." Jesus sent multitudes away and drew apart to pray. If it was necessary for Him, how much more so is it necessary for us who are so much weaker than He.

If we do not voluntarily take time for God, sometimes He forces Himself upon us. The disciples saw no necessity for prayer, so Jesus made them get into the boat. But solitude was not enough. Then we read that a storm came upon them and their ship was "tossed with waves." Mark tells us they "toiled in rowing; for the wind was contrary unto them" (Mark 6:48)

They were in a situation they could not handle. Their

strength was not sufficient to carry them where they wanted to go. I think God sent that storm upon the disciples. Sometimes God puts us on our backs to give us a chance to look up.

WHEN GOD WAITS

Does God send the trials and difficulties into our lives? Certainly not in every case. Often our suffering is caused by our own stupidity and our wrong acts. Sometimes our suffering is brought about through the faults of others. But sometimes God is a disturbing God who will not let us rest.

We remember how Jonah refused to answer God's call. Instead he took a ship to Tarshish. On board the ship, Jonah became complacent and went to sleep, though he was steadily moving away from God and duty. Though He was forgotten, God did not forget and we read, "The Lord sent out a great wind into the sea" (Jonah 1:4). Rutherford translates that: "The Lord hurled a storm at Jonah." And when the disciples were about to lose their heads and go off with the crowd, Jesus made them get into the ship and God sent a storm. They rowed with all their strength but they could make no progress against the wind.

Has your life ever been upset? Have circumstances been so against you that though you struggled with all your strength, you could make no progress? If so, you are interested in this story. Jesus had gone alone out into the mountains to pray—yet He was not alone. God was there and in that fellowship He found strength and peace. But not only was the power of God present when He prayed, also on His heart were the needs of men.

Out on the mountainside He could see that storm. He knew the thoughts of His disciples out there. He watched them struggle. He waited. God wants to come into our lives but He watches and waits until we need Him. As long as we feel sufficient unto ourselves we are our own god and we have no place for Him. So Jesus waited until "the fourth watch of the night"—three o'clock in the morning. They say it is darkest just before dawn and it was not until then that the disciples were ready to receive Him.

We remember the Psalmist said: "Yea, though I walk through the valley of the shadow of death, I will fear no evil: for thou art with me" (Ps. 23). Often until we pass through some valley of the shadow we never realize His presence.

At the proper moment Jesus left the shelter of the mountainside and went walking out across the water into the storm to where those in need were. And to them He said, "Be of good cheer."

We think of Jesus' walking on the water as the miracle of this story. But the real miracle is the fact that He knows our situation. He also knows our hearts. And He always comes at the right moment. Someone expressed this story in a little song:

Just when I need Him, Jesus is near;
Just when I falter, just when I fear,
Ready to help me, ready to cheer,
Just when I need Him most;
Jesus is near to comfort and cheer,
Just when I need Him most.

Thousands can testify to that fact and that is the real miracle.

How Jesus comes is incidental. He may come walking across the water, or through the inspiration of a church service, or through the help of some friend, or through some change in the circumstances of your life, or in one of many ways. The important thing is that when we feel the need of Him and are ready to receive Him, He knows it and always comes.

STOP LOOKING AT THE WIND

When Simon Peter saw Jesus walking across the water in the midst of the storm, he was so inspired that he jumped out of the boat and began walking across the water to meet Jesus. But before he walked far he began to sink. In explanation of his sinking the Bible says, "When he saw the wind."

There is an experience that most of us have had. Under the power of some great inspiration we have undertaken that which ordinarily would seem impossible. And for a time we have succeeded but then we begin to sink. What has happened? "When he saw the wind." We dare to launch forth because of some high dream and the vision of a great goal. But we lose sight of the goal and begin to consider the difficulties. When that happens we lose our power.

Do you remember the journey of the children of Israel through the wilderness? They were kept going by their vision of The Promised Land. And on the border of that land they stopped. For a generation they were denied the land, but not because they could not possess it—later they did take it. They stopped because there were giants in the way, and instead of looking at the land, they concentrated on the giants. When we think of our problems instead of our powers we always begin to sink.

I was talking with a man whose work requires him to climb to the top of those high television towers. I asked him how he kept from getting dizzy and falling. He said, "As I climb I always keep looking up." As long as Simon Peter kept his eyes on Christ he could walk. But when he turned from the source of his strength and began considering his difficulties he was lost.

Here is the explanation of St. Paul's amazing confidence. He said, "I can do all things through Christ which strengtheneth me" (Phil. 4:13). If Paul had fixed his mind on the forces against him and on the power of Rome, he would have quit even before he started. But because he held his gaze steadily on Christ he never faltered. Whatever task Paul faced he said, "I can." The picture of Christ in our minds gives us that assurance.

Put a plank on the ground and no one of us would have difficulty in walking it. Lift the same plank high in the air and most of us would shrink from even trying to walk it. The plank is just as wide in the air as it is on the ground. The difference is that when it is in the air we think about falling rather than walking. And we usually do what we think about.

Even by our prayers we often make our situation worse. We fill our minds with our needs instead of with Him who can supply those needs. We concentrate on our weakness instead of His strength. We look at our sins instead of our Saviour. We think of our problems instead of His power.

As Peter began to sink he looked up again and he cried, "Lord, save me." Then we read, "Immediately Jesus stretched forth his hand." No matter how desperate our situation, Jesus is both ready and able to save us when by faith we look to Him. I cannot explain how He does, but in company with thousands of others I can testify to the fact that He does it.

16. DID JESUS REALLY CURSE A FIG TREE?

The Miracle of the Fig Tree

MATTHEW 21:18-22

JESUS HAD spent the night out in the country. Coming back into the city the next morning He saw a fig tree, and being hungry He went down to it to get some figs to eat. But He found it had nothing but leaves so He said, "Let no fruit grow on thee henceforward forever." The tree withered away.

The disciples marveled at the fig tree withering. To them Jesus pointed out that if one has faith he can move mountains—if one prays he shall receive. The value of a fig tree lies in the fruit it produces—the value of faith and prayer are the results they bring. To Christ, religion was something of real, practical value, not something just beautiful and decorative.

The greatest temptation of religion is to become worship-centered instead of service-centered. A lady came late to the church one day and asked the janitor, "Is the service over?" He made an inspired reply: "Lady, the worship is over but the service has just begun." That should be true of every experience of worship, but the danger lies in the fact that we can satisfy ourselves with just the act of worship.

After Jesus and some of His disciples had that great spiritual experience on the Mount of Transfiguration, Peter wanted to stay there. But Jesus led them back down into the valley. There they found a boy who needed help. To those who had tried to help the boy but had failed Jesus said, "This kind can come forth by nothing, but by prayer and fasting" (Mark 9:29). Service without power gained through worship is inadequate, but worship which does not express itself in service is worthless.

The particular species of fig tree which Jesus saw was supposed to have fruit when it had leaves, but this tree had nothing but leaves. Jesus condemns to death the principle of life without fruit. Madame Chiang Kai-shek said, "Confucianism worships ancestors but never built an old folks' home." Such a religion is no better than a fig tree gone to leaf.

Once a soap manufacturer was arguing with a minister about the value of religion. He named a number of instances of wickedness and corruption in the world and said that religion had not done any good. About that time a little boy, who had been playing in the mud, came walking by. The minister observed, "Neither has soap done any good because there are still dirty people in the world." The manufacturer replied, "Soap is of no value unless it is applied." "Exactly," answered the minister, "and the same is true of religion."

I read about a boy whose father's will provided that he was to receive $2,000 per year as long as he was in college. The boy continued in college for forty-six years and when he died he had eleven degrees, but his education was no good because he never used it. And there are people who have spent a lifetime reading their Bibles, praying and going to church, but they never actually used their religion. And that Jesus condemns.

THE SIN OF USELESSNESS

Did Jesus use His power to curse a fig tree? As we study His life we see how He used His power to heal and to save and never to hurt. He spoke kindly to sinners and was ever ready to forgive. But the one thing our Lord warned against the most was uselessness. He spoke many parables illustrating the judgment of God, and many were condemned to eternal death, but in no parable was one flung out into the darkness because of some positive wrong.

Jesus told about Dives who went to hell. As far as the record goes, he didn't steal or cheat. He just failed to help the poor man at his gate. There was the rich farmer who lost his soul. He worked hard but he failed to use the fruits of his labor for any worthwhile service. Jesus had contempt for the priest and the Levite. They did not rob or beat the man who was wounded. They just passed him by.

There was the servant who was cast into "outer darkness." He did not use in wrongful ways the talent entrusted to him. He simply buried it in the ground and did nothing with it. Jesus told about the five virgins in whose faces the door was shut. It wasn't because they had become unclean. It was because their lamps were not burning. And as Jesus stood before the fig tree—a tree that was supposed to have fruit but had only leaves —He condemned it to death.

Once He said, "Think not that I am come to destroy the law, or the prophets: I am come not to destroy, but to fulfill" (Matt. 5:17). And one of the fundamental laws of life is that only the useful things survive. Squirrels have bushy tails because they are useful for balancing on the limbs of trees. Dogs and cats have eyes in the front of their heads because they are hunters and need to keep the game they chase in sight. Rabbits have eyes in the side of their heads because they are not hunters but are hunted, and they need to watch in every direction for approaching enemies. The things we use for our good, we keep.

The animal has a marvelous sense of smell but people are losing theirs. The animal uses his for survival but the human increasingly depends on other senses. And that which we do not use eventually dies. Put your arm in a tight sling, keep it inactive, and after awhile it will wither away. There are fish in Mammoth Cave that are totally blind. They still have eyes but have lived in total darkness so long they have lost their sight.

And so it is with a human life. God made us for a purpose. I believe no person is here by accident. Jesus said, "As my father hath sent me, even so send I you" (John 20:21). Surely we believe the purpose of every life is to be fruitful. And when a person fails in his mission he withers and dies.

Study, as I have so many times, the lives of people who are "fed up" with living and you will find that they are failing to bear any real fruit. "He that loseth his life for my sake shall find it," said Christ (Matt. 10:39). You never live until you begin to live for something.

NO FRUIT, WE DIE

Recently I spent nearly a week in a little cottage far back in the mountains. I never enjoyed anything in my life as much as I enjoyed the first two days there. I went to bed at dark and slept for ten hours. I sat on the porch and looked at the beautiful mountains. I was several miles away from a telephone. No newspaper was delivered to my door. Nobody came around to see me. There was no mail to answer.

But after a couple of days I caught up on my sleep and I got restless. I walked around through the woods, but just walking without going anywhere didn't appeal to me very long. I wanted something to do. I wanted to be with other people. God did not make us just to enjoy His world. He made us to work in His world. And in the sharing with Him of the continual creation we find our life. When we cease to be a part of the creative work of God we soon die.

One day Jesus condemned a fig tree to death because it produced no fruit. Some people seemed shocked that Christ would use His power for destructive purposes. But such is the very basic law of life. When we cease to bear fruit we die.

Only a few days ago a friend of mine expressed concern for my health. He asked if I had not recently lost some weight. (Incidentally, people have been asking me that same question for twenty-five years. I have not lost any weight because I have never had any to lose.) Then this friend mentioned the things I am trying to do and very mournfully predicted I would not live until I was fifty years old.

I don't know how long I will live. Neither does anyone else. But one thing I do know—I am living now. And that is more than some people can say. I once buried a young soldier who was killed while leading his men up a hill during a battle. His mother was crushed that he had died so young. But I pointed out to her that he probably packed more real living into the thirty minutes he used in climbing that hill than some people put into seventy years.

The unhappiest people in the world are the ones who are living within themselves. I sympathize with the little boy who was so lonely he said to his mother, "I wish I were two little puppies so I could play together."

Let me stop—stop dead still for a moment—and ask myself this question: "Is there a single soul who would look me square in the eye and say, 'I thank God for you. My life is better because of you. I am glad you are living—' would anybody say that to me?" If you were to die tonight, would it be much of a loss to anybody? Would it really?

What is the answer to the fruitless life? Not in some

feverish activity or a lot of little services. Before we do our best, we must first be our best. And the first step is right relationship with God. Let us pray:

Take my life, and let it be
Consecrated Lord, to Thee.

17. HOW TO DO A LOT WITH A LITTLE

The Miracle of Feeding Five Thousand

MATTHEW 14:13-21; MARK 6:30-44;
LUKE 9:10-17; JOHN 6:1-13

THERE ARE more than thirty separate miracles of Christ which are recorded in one or more of the four gospels but only one of those miracles is recorded by all four of the gospel writers. It is the story of the feeding of the five thousand. No doubt this miracle made more impression on the people than any other miracle of our Lord's.

Let's look at the story. Jesus and His disciples were tired and He suggested they get off by themselves and rest awhile. The story says, "there were many coming and going," and nothing wears a person down like the constant movements in a crowd. Especially do I notice this in a city. I spend several weeks each year preaching in small towns. The people are less hurried, more rested and more confident. Much of the nervous tension people have today is simply because they are tired. Any person is more nervous and irritable when he has not had a chance to relax and rest. Our Lord was anxious to win the world but He also knew one must be willing to take time off.

Long before life was so complicated and noisy as it is today, God commanded the people to take one day in seven for worship and the recreation of their souls. We are in danger of throwing that commandment out. Sir James Chrichton Browne, a famous physician, said, "We doctors, in the treatment of nervous disease, are now constantly compelled to prescribe periods of rest. Such periods are, I think, only Sundays in arrears."

I would like to dwell on this point because I know nothing this modern generation needs more than to learn how to relax serenely. Like the old woman said, in explaining her long life, "I have learned to sit loose." It is well to remember that if you never learn to let go, there will come a time when you cannot hang on. We need to pray with Augustine: "Let my soul take refuge from the crowding turmoil of world thoughts beneath the shadow of Thy wings." Jesus showed us how to "take up a Cross." He also showed us how to relax. The two go hand in hand. "Come ye yourselves apart into a desert place, and rest awhile," He said.

But as they went, the people saw them and came in great numbers. No doubt the word was quickly spread around into the surrounding towns and a crowd of five thousand gathered. When Jesus saw them He was "moved with compassion." He saw their needs and He was concerned to help them. I think that is why the multitudes came to Christ. I know He had the power to work great miracles and could speak as no man ever spoke. But more important, He loved people and they responded to Him. He began to teach and to heal and to inspire their souls. But there came a time when they needed physical food. Sometimes we think religion is only concerned with "pie in the sky," while we are compelled to be concerned with "bread on earth." Let us remember that our Lord who taught us to pray, "Give us this day our daily bread," was willing, even eager, to use His marvelous power to provide for the everyday physical needs of the multitude.

It is good for me to pray about the salvation of my soul. It is just as much in order for me to ask God to help me get a job or to bless my business. And the God who made blue birds and violets surely wants us to have not only the bare necessities, but also some of the lovely luxuries. Not only is He anxious for us to have bread, but also He is glad when we have some cake.

CHRIST KNEW WHAT TO DO

In the story of the feeding of the five thousand, when the multitude grew hungry all the disciples could think of was "Send them away." After all, there were five thousand of them, and the disciples had no food or money. That is a very human situation in which we frequently find ourselves. We come face to face with some situation we do not have resources to meet, so instead of doing what we can, we "pass the buck."

Sometimes if we cannot put the responsibility on someone else, we seek to escape it by running away ourselves. Even the Psalmist once said: "Oh that I had wings like a dove! for then would I fly away, and be at rest" (Ps. 55:6). Sometimes people become so anxious to escape the situation of life in which they are that they are even willing to destroy their own lives. A man came to me recently who was very much disturbed over the fact that he had felt an inclination to suicide. I told him that most people have at one time or another had a fleeting desire to "end it all."

Perhaps the most common practice in the face of a need we feel unable to meet is to put it off. We have a way of waiting until tomorrow for a more convenient season. But life slips quietly along carrying our opportunities forever beyond our reach. We can put it off so long that eventually we have missed out in the great adventure of living.

One thing the disciples overlooked. They were correct in feeling they were up against a great need, but they failed to consider their own resources and they also failed to consider the power of God. There is never a situation that we and God together cannot handle.

In the face of that hungry multitude, it never occurred to Christ to "send them away." John tells us, "He Himself knew what He would do." God always has a plan to meet every situation. No emergency ever takes God by surprise. There are those who believe that God's only plan for this world is to desert it and to destroy it. But He is not that kind of a God. God's plan was to establish His Kingdom here, and in spite of super-bombs and Russian aggression He will not be defeated. He made each of us for a purpose, and if we let Him work with us we will not finally be defeated.

So Christ said to those anxious, defeated disciples, "How many loaves have you?" That is, before you give up take stock of your resources. Maybe you do not have enough to see you through, but you will discover you have enough to start on. Andrew, one of the disciples, said, "There is a lad here with five barley loaves and two small fishes." That is fine. I feel like shouting, "Good for you, Andrew." But then he ruins it. He feebly throws up his hands and asks, "But what are they among so many?" How many talents and resources of ours have we wasted simply by saying, "It isn't enough even to start with?"

I wish we knew more about that lad, who he was and what became of him. I wonder how he felt when they asked him to give up his lunch. After all, he was hungry too. But when Christ asked him for all the loaves and fishes he had, the boy gave them. And the marvelous thing is that not only were they used for the blessing of many, many other people, but in the end the boy also had enough and even more. I know people whose lives God could take and use in effective ways, but they selfishly hold on and hold back. What a blessing it is to a person when he realizes he never loses what he consecrates to God's use.

CHRIST GAVE THANKS FOR WHAT HE HAD

In the story of the feeding of the five thousand by Christ, notice carefully the steps He took. First, He recognized the need. The people were hungry and should be fed. Second, He took stock of the available resources. All they could find was a lad with five loaves and two fishes. So Christ used that. Third, and this is an important step, He took the loaves and gave thanks. That is simply marvelous.

I wish I were an artist. I would like to paint four pictures and hang them where I would see them every day. Not being able to paint those pictures on canvas, I have made an effort to put them clearly on the screen of my mind. The first picture shows five thousand hungry people. Standing in their midst is He who always is concerned about human need. In His hands is the little boy's lunch. He might have complained about having so little when He needed so much. Instead of complaining, He lifts up His eyes to God and gives thanks.

The next picture shows this same Christ at a table with twelve men. It seemed that everything was lost and nothing had been gained. In His hand is a piece of bread which He will use as an example of His body and how it will be broken. He might have become panicky or bitter. Instead, the Bible tells us, "He took bread, and gave thanks" (Luke 22:19).

The third picture shows a ship in the midst of a raging storm at sea. On board were two hundred and seventy-six people. For fourteen days they had been blown by the storm and now it seemed they might be dashed on the rocks. They were terrified. Then Paul stood up and before the people "took bread, and gave thanks to God" (Acts 27:35).

The fourth picture shows a little band of people who had just the year before come to America, a new and a strange land. During that year half of their families had died. They were facing a hard winter in New England. Savages were all about them. They had produced a very meager harvest. But in spite of their hard experiences, they knelt to thank God for their blessings.

I wish every person who complains could see those pictures. I wish they could be seen by those who have given up and quit, feeling their resources to be insufficient for their needs, and also by those who are in trouble, or those who have suffered and lost. There is marvelous power in the experience of genuine thanksgiving.

After giving thanks, without waiting for the bread to be multiplied, Jesus began to break it. What a great faith! He began by using what He had and to the amazement of the people, He had sufficient for all their needs. In fact, there were twelve baskets of food left over.

How the bread was multiplied I cannot explain. It is a miracle. But it is a miracle that is repeated again and again. It can even be repeated in your own life. No matter what your need might be or how badly the circumstances of life have run against you, if you will take what resources you have, be truly thankful for what you have and begin to use that, you will find that God will add His power and you will have all you need, even more. Begin acting on that faith and you will see.

18. THE CAUSE AND CURE OF FEAR

The Miracle of Stilling the Tempest

MARK 4:35-41

"WHY ARE YE SO fearful?" Nearly two thousand years ago that question was asked by Christ of a group of men in a storm. If Christ were on earth in the flesh today, that same question would be upon His lips.

Speaking of the cave men, Lewis Browne said, "In the beginning there was fear; and fear was in the heart of man and fear controlled man. At every turn it whelmed over him, leaving him no moment of ease. With the wild soughing of the wind, with the crashing of the thunder and the growling of lurking beasts, fear swept through him. All the days of man were gray with fear, because all his universe seemed charged with danger, and he, poor, gibbering, half-ape, nursing his wounds in some draughty cave, could only tremble with fear."

Well, we have developed in many ways since the days of the cave man. Today we can measure the force of the wind and explain the thunder. We have means of protection against the lurking beasts of our day. We are not living in draughty caves but in comfortable homes. We know much and we have achieved much and we are proud of our culture and civilization. But still, like the cave man of old, we are trembling with fear. Why? "Why are ye so fearful?" Christ would ask today.

A generation ago a British publishing firm issued a book under the title, *If I Could Preach Only Once*. A number of men were asked to write the sermon they would preach if they had just one opportunity. One of those sermons was written by Gilbert Chesterton, a very wise and clever man. He said, "If I could preach only one sermon, it would be a sermon against fear." Certainly his thinking is in line with the Christian faith.

We remember that God sent a messenger from Heaven to announce the birth of the Saviour. That angel had only one opportunity to preach and we note that the very first words of that sermon were "Fear not" (Luke 2:10). The worst enemy of your life is perverted fear. I say perverted because basically fear is good. God made man with the capacity to be afraid for man's own protection. Only a fool is fearless. Because a student fears an examination, he prepares for it. We read, "The fear of the Lord is the beginning of knowledge" (Prov. 1:7). Fear develops humility, reverence and faith.

But when fear is perverted it becomes a monster which paralyzes and destroys one's life. We remember the story Jesus told of the man who buried his talent in the ground. "I was afraid," he said. His talent was taken away from him and he was called an unprofitable servant (Matt. 25:25-30). And today there are vast numbers of people whose lives are "unprofitable" simply because they are paralyzed by fear.

In his book, *The Conquest of Fear,* Basil King pointed out that fear causes more misery than all the sin and sickness of our lives combined. We are not sick all the time. We are not sinning all the time. But most people are afraid of something or somebody—all the time.

"Why are ye so fearful?" asked Christ.

FAITH CONQUERS FEAR

Jesus and His disciples were on a boat crossing the sea of Galilee. Suddenly a storm came up, with waves running so high that the water came into the ship. The ship was not big enough to cope with the storm. No doubt the disciples worked with all their strength, but they also were insufficient to meet the storm. They became afraid. Why? Because they felt their resources were so little in comparison to the storm that they were going to be sunk.

That is exactly why any person is afraid. He feels that he is unequal to the life which he is forced to face. Now what is the cure for that fear? Jesus said, "How is it that ye have no faith?" The only cure for fear is faith. In the midst of that storm, why was not Jesus afraid? Because He knew He had the power to overcome that storm.

A young man was telling me recently that any day he might lose his job. But he told me he was not the least bit worried about it. He knew that due to his training and ability he could quickly get another job. He had faith in himself and he was not afraid. A person may be sick and become afraid he is going to die. But the doctor comes, and after examination, tells the patient what his trouble is. Also the doctor assures him that he has had many like cases which were cured. The doctor prescribes a treatment and says the patient will be well soon. The sick man loses his fear because he has faith in the doctor.

You never develop fear until after you have lost your confidence. And the extent of your confidence is determined by the extent of your faith. You are not afraid that you won't get back home tonight. You know the way and you think your car will not break down. Even if you got lost on some unfamiliar street, you know you can ask someone for directions. If your car should break down, you know you can get help.

But life often gets us into places where we don't know the way, or into situations where our resources are insufficient. And we know of nobody we can call on for help. Even if we do not actually get into that condition, we know it might happen and just the mere possibility gives fear the chance to grow wild in our minds and drive us to dread and even panic.

The basis of fear is the possibility of failure. The power of faith is the assurance of success. Emerson said, "They can conquer who believe they can." We don't get faith as a result of our victories; rather we gain the victories because of our faith.

THREEFOLD KNOWLEDGE OF GOD

As Christ stood on the deck of a storm-tossed little ship, surrounded by a group of fearful men, calmly He said, "Peace, be still." The winds and the waves were immediately quiet. Also, the fears of the men were gone. Not only were their fears of that particular storm conquered, but also their fears of the future storms. They knew that as long as they had Christ with them they need not be afraid of a storm.

Long before, the Psalmist learned that same truth. He said, "Yea though I walk through the valley of the shadow of death." That refers not just to the experience of death but to any crisis one might be called upon to face. "I will fear no evil." Why? "For thou art with me."

Now this faith does not mean that every time a storm arises we can call on God and He will immediately quiet it. Sometimes Christ says to the winds and the waves, "Peace, be still." But at other times He says it to the person. Sometimes He changes our situation; at other times He changes us. Sometimes He removes the mountain from our path; at other times He enables us to walk over the mountains.

Certainly the greatest Christian this world has ever known was St. Paul. In his life were storms of every description and very rarely were the storms told to be still. Instead, St. Paul developed an inner strength that was stronger than any storm. He said, "I can do all things through Christ which strengtheneth me" (Phil. 4:13). He knew that no storm could defeat him, so he had no reason to worry or to be afraid. Paul's faith overcame his fears.

In order to have fear-conquering faith, Dr. Fosdick has well pointed out that we must come to know God in three ways. A musician might study the compositions of Beethoven until he learns them. Then he knows Beethoven the composer. This musician might have heard Beethoven play and as a result come to know him not only as a composer but also as a performer. He might have known him in still a third way, that is by personal acquaintance and through companionship and friendship. But no one really knew the great Beethoven until he knew him in all three ways.

The Psalmist said, "The heavens declare the glory of God" (Ps. 19:1). Through study of this world, many people have come to believe in God the creator, or composer. But Christians came to know God in another way. They became acquainted with Christ and the life He lived on earth. As we see Him, we know God the performer. Now there is still a third way to know God and that is through His Spiritual Presence. Through the experience of the Spirit, we know God in still a third way.

So at the conclusion of a service St. Paul would say: "The grace of the Lord Jesus Christ, and the love of God, and the communion of the Holy Spirit, be with you all. Amen" (II Cor. 13:14).

19. WHY DOES GOD WAIT TO ANSWER OUR PRAYERS?

The Miracle of Raising Lazarus from the Dead

JOHN 11:1-46

———————

I GET A NEW thrill every time I read the story of Jesus and Lazarus. It has love, pathos, drama and builds up to a climax so grand that it includes both earth and heaven. It begins with Lazarus who was sick. So many of the stories in the life of Christ begin with the needs of some person. In truth, that is where most of us begin with Christ. We have a need we cannot meet and we then look to Him who is able to supply our every need.

The two sisters, Mary and Martha, sent word to Him, saying, "Lord, he whom thou lovest is sick." What a marvelous lesson in prayer! First, when trouble came they wanted Christ to know about it. And through the centuries, as unnumbered multitudes of people have become frightened or burdened, they have instinctively reached through the darkness to feel for the hand of Christ. Somehow we know He will be concerned.

My heart is stirred daily as I get letters from people I have never seen telling me their troubles. The only contact many of these have ever had with me is reading my articles in a big metropolitan newspaper. But their hearts have become burdened and they had no one to tell it to who really cared. I read those letters with a special prayer in my heart.

Mary and Martha were also showing a marvelous faith. They had a great need—they told Christ about it— they felt that that was sufficient. They did not feel it

108

necessary to tell Him what to do. They had faith to believe that He would do the right thing. In our prayers we would do well to have as much faith. "He whom thou lovest is sick." A short prayer, yet it contains all that is necessary.

Now notice Christ's strange reaction to their prayer. As you read the Gospels, you are impressed with His eagerness to help those who came for His help. He was never too busy. No person was ever turned away. So when the word came about Lazarus, you might expect to read how He hurried to Bethany to the bedside of Lazarus. Or better still, he might have just spoken the word as He did on behalf of the Centurion's servant, and healed Lazarus at the very moment. So we are surprised to read, "He abode two days still in the same place where he was."

I can picture those two anxious sisters. They kept walking to and fro from the bedside of their loved to the window. "Why doesn't He come?" they would wonder in anguish. "Surely He will be here any moment now," one would say to comfort the other. But darkness came and He wasn't there. All through the night they watched and waited but still He didn't come. Another day slowly dragged by and still another night. Finally Lazarus died, and still He hadn't come.

That is the hardest part of prayer. If God says "No," we can accept it. If He says "Yes," we are glad. But when God keeps saying "Wait," we find that hardest to bear. And sometimes it does seem that God waits too long. But He doesn't. The old prophet was right when he said, "If the vision tarry, wait for it, for it will come, and it will not be late" (Hab. 2:3).

LAZARUS DIED

Why did Christ allow Lazarus to die? If we can answer that, maybe it will give us the answer to why God has allowed some of the pain, sorrow and suffering that you have had to bear. Recently I have been praying especially for a dear lady suffering day and night with arthritis. Why is God delaying the answer?

Certainly Christ knew about Lazarus' being sick. Also he knew of the worry and anguish in the heart of Mary and Martha. Sometimes we think God is not aware of our sorrows and needs. We may doubt that He even hears our prayers. But Jesus assures us that God even notes the fall of one little sparrow. Jesus knew of the seriousness of Lazarus' condition, yet He did nothing about it. Why?

It was not because He was unable to heal Lazarus. As you study His life you see He was able to heal even lepers, to make the cripple walk, the deaf hear and the blind see. Even the winds and waves obeyed His voice. We sometimes doubt God's ability to meet our particular situation. Thus we cease to pray and to look to Him. But God is always sufficient. With just one word Christ could have saved Lazarus. Why didn't He do it?

Sometimes we believe that our suffering is a sign that God is angry with us and wants to punish us. We may doubt His love for us. But such was not the case with Lazarus. The story begins with the love of Christ for him. "He whom thou lovest is sick," they said. And it has seemed to me that some who have suffered the most have been those who loved God the most. Notice the story says, "Now Jesus loved Martha, and her sister, and Lazarus."

He loved them, not as a family, but one by one. We must remember that God's love is always an individual love. Jesus was constantly dealing with the one person.

THE TOUCH OF THE MASTER'S HAND

Some of His greatest utterances were to individuals. He healed one by one. We talk about "mass" evangelism, but He talked about the shepherd going out after the one sheep. He loved this one man who was sick. Then why did He let him die?

I don't know. I just do not know. I say with St. Paul, "For now we see through a glass, darkly." But I also say with Paul, "but then face to face: now I know in part; but then shall I know even as also I am known" (I Cor. 13:12). If we knew all the answers, we would not need faith. Faith takes up where sight leaves off. The Bible says, "Now faith is . . . the evidence of things not seen" (Heb. 11:1). Faith pierces the darkness of our hearts and knows there is an answer, a reason—a good reason—and it accepts that fact and keeps moving toward God.

Lazarus did die. Then we read, "Many of the Jews came to Martha and Mary, to comfort them." So many things on this earth have changed—the clothes we wear, the food we eat, even the language we speak—but people are still the same. When a heart is broken, friends still come to sympathize, to comfort. And what a blessing it is to have someone to share our sorrows. Sometimes a friend who cares means more than anything else on earth.

MARTHA STILL BELIEVED

When Jesus finally came to Bethany where Lazarus had died, we read that "Martha, as soon as she heard that Jesus was coming, went and met him." That is wonderful. While her brother was sick she had sent word to Christ and had expected Him to do something. Instead, He delayed coming until it seemed it was now too late. Death had beat Him there. Yet in spite of that Martha was not bitter.

She might have said, "I refuse ever to speak to Christ again. He failed me when I asked His help." But be it to her everlasting glory, she didn't say that. In my years as a minister I have come to know people in almost every condition. Many will bring tears of sympathy to your eyes. But the most pitiful, hopeless creature I have ever met is one who has allowed a sorrow to make him bitter. I am praying for a man now who said to me, "God could have saved me from this. He didn't, and I will never darken the door of a church again."

Not only did Jesus fail to save Lazarus, He didn't even come to the funeral. He was their best friend. He could have come but He didn't. Their neighbors came. They sent flowers. They helped in every way they could. But Jesus didn't come. Still Martha was so anxious to see Him that she ran out to meet Him. We love her for that spirit.

Her first words to Him were: "If thou hadst been here, my brother had not died." Many times we feel that our troubles are a sign that God has forgotten us. Sometimes our troubles do come because God was not with us. Many couples can say, "Lord, if thou hadst been in our home, it would not have been broken." Many defeated, miserable people can say, "Lord, if thou hadst been in my life, things would have been different." But in cases like that, the reason of His absence was because we refused to let Him come in. God never forsakes us. We forsake Him.

Now notice the complete faith of Martha: "Even now, whatsoever thou wilt ask of God, God will give it thee." It is so easy to lose hope and throw up our hands in despair. But we need to know that with Christ no person is hopeless. With Christ there is a solution to every problem. With Christ something can always be done. We only become hopeless when we refuse to believe.

Every Sunday night I ask my congregation to sing the little chorus: "Only believe, only believe; all things are possible, only believe." God's power in our lives is limited only by our lack of belief. What is your situation? Remember the faith of Martha—even when death had come, she still believed Christ could do something. We have a saying, "Where there is life, there is hope," but Martha goes even beyond that. She had hoped even in death. At least we do have life and we should know that no matter what has happened, when we pray it will bring results.

Jesus said to her, "Thy brother shall rise again." To you He will say, There is still life ahead. May we rise to that faith.

20. FOR THOSE WHO WANT LIFE INSTEAD OF DEATH

The Miracle of Raising Lazarus from the Dead

JOHN 11:1-46

MARTHA'S HEART was broken because of the death of her brother, Lazarus. To her Jesus said, "Thy brother shall rise again," but that gave her very little comfort. She said, "I know that he shall rise again in the resurrection at the last day," but to her that was so far away. And the final resurrection seems so strange and vague.

Then Jesus said to her the most beautiful and comforting word that has ever been spoken in the presence of death: "I am the resurrection, and the life: he that believeth in me, though he were dead, yet shall he live: and whosoever liveth and believeth in me shall never die."

To comment on those words of our Lord is like trying to describe a rainbow or a sunset. Human words are so inadequate. You can't describe in words the sound of a gentle breeze rustling through the trees on a hot summer day, or the melody of a pipe organ, or the beauty of a rose, or the depth of a mother's love. In those words Christ reveals the glorious truth that it is possible for a human being to be forever beyond the reach of death.

Suppose some physician were to make a discovery that would put every person beyond the reach of cancer. The news would be proclaimed joyously around the world. Think about how that announcement would immediately take so much fear and dread out of our minds. I have talked with many people who suspected they might have cancer. The very suspicion so filled them with fear that they would not go to a doctor. I have seen others just give up and die when they learned they had cancer. The cancer did not kill them. Just the fear of it was enough.

And there are people who can hardly stand to hear the word death spoken. They live in such mortal dread of it that even the life they have is no joy. But the Son of God has come to tell us that death can be eliminated, and vast multitudes believe what He said. Why do we crowd our churches on Easter? We talk about the Easter parade, but new clothes are not the answer. On that day we come to church in large numbers because from Christ we have the assurance that death has been conquered.

A minister was talking to me about the competition of the television with the church on Sunday night. At the church hour, a program comes out of New York that costs $60,000 to put on. The people can sit in their homes and see it. No church has that much money to spend on a single service.

Yet, he pointed out, the church does compete—not

because it has more money to spend, but rather because it has something more valuable to offer. In the field of entertainment the church is left far behind, but in having a Christ who is the answer to death the church stands before thirsty people like a cool spring in the midst of a desert. As long as people desire life instead of death, they will come to Christ.

THE DEAD SHALL LIVE

Jesus said to Martha, "I am the resurrection, and the life: he that believeth in me, though he were dead, yet shall he live: and whosoever liveth and believeth in me shall never die." There He is saying two things: (1) the dead shall live again; (2) the living shall never die.

"Though he were dead," our Lord said. There is such a thing as death. There are numbers of people walking the streets of any city who are dead. Do you remember when you were in your youth? Life was thrilling, songs and laughter filled your mind, you had high purposes and lofty ambitions. You were gloriously alive.

Little by little, however, as you grew older you settled down. Setbacks and disappointments came along. There was the old daily routine and the struggle to make a living. The very monotony of a lot of people's existence is a deadening thing. Before we realize it, we find ourselves in a rut. You know what a rut is? It is a grave with the ends knocked out—an endless grave. A lot of people are now buried in some rut.

Hopes can die, dreams can die, ideals can die. We remember the Bible tells us, "The soul that sinneth, it shall die" (Ezek. 18:4). St. Paul warned that "The wages of sin is death" (Rom. 6:23). We have a way of telling ourselves that a little sin doesn't hurt. We soothe and ease our conscience and we are told, "Don't worry about it." But let us never forget that sin and wrong can bring death inside of us. Then we become bodies without souls.

Study history and you will find that no civilization has ever been destroyed by an invading army or an outside enemy. But civilizations have died from the inside. Read again the story of Babylon. The city was so well fortified that no enemy could attack it. In the vaults were gold and silver and precious jewels beyond calculation. The people there felt safe and secure.

One night Belshazzar had a great banquet. He had the sacred vessels brought from the temple and desecrated them. A hand appeared on the wall and began to write, "MENE, MENE, TEKEL, U-PHARSIN." He did not know what it meant so he sent for Daniel, the preacher. Daniel interpreted them for him, "Thou art weighed in the balances and found wanting."

Babylon had lost its moral fiber; it leveled out the high and holy places and nothing remained sacred. When that happens either to a nation or to a person, it brings death. During the last war when France surrendered, Churchill said, "England has lost her buildings but France has lost her soul." And there are people who are getting along pretty well financially whose souls have died.

Even for those Christ is sufficient. "He that believeth in me, though he were dead, yet shall he live." In Korea they call a Christian a "resurrected" person. Accepting Christ as your Saviour is not some little moral reform, it is a new birth and a new life.

THE LIVING SHALL NEVER DIE

Jesus said, "Whosoever liveth and believeth in me shall never die." That is the most glorious promise ever made to humanity. We go to the cemetery. It is a sacred spot which we bathe with our tears, but our loved are

not there. They never have been there. They never will
be there. You bury only things that are dead, and Christ
assures us that through Him we will never die. The
body dies and is buried. The person does not die and
therefore is not buried.

We remember the words of our Lord to the man
dying by His side that day. He said, "Today shalt thou
be with me in paradise" (Luke 23:43). Not in some
dim, distant future—today. Not at some general resurrection—today. Not when some Gabriel blows a horn—
today. Our life will not cease and start over again. It
continues on in another place. The very moment we
leave this body we begin living in the next life.

When I conduct a funeral I usually say to the family
that it is both a time of sadness and rejoicing. When a
loved one's body dies it breaks our hearts and fills our
eyes with tears. We would not have it otherwise. There
is something wrong with a person who can be physically
separated from one he truly loved and not feel deep
sorrow. It always leaves a hurt in our hearts that will
never be healed. Sorrow because of death is not a lack
of faith. Though we have complete confidence in the future life, still the separation is hard to bear.

Have you ever been on a college campus on the
opening day of school? Proudly the parents drive up
with their boy or girl. They help get the things to the
room and are happy to see their child entering college
and a larger life. But if you watch, you will see a mama
quickly wipe some tears away when she thinks no one is
looking. Even papa feels a little moisture in his eyes and
he tells his child good-bye. It is both a time of sadness
and of joy.

Certainly one of the happiest occasions of all is a
wedding. We want our children to marry, but it is a rare
mother who doesn't shed some tears even though it is a
happy time. We want our children to go away to college

and to marry, but the separation comes hard. And to a much greater extent is that true when a loved one enters the Father's House. We do believe and we are confident they have entered a better life. But even that assurance does not keep us from feeling lonely without the physical presence of one we love.

After Jesus had given the assurance to Martha of life eternal, we read that she went to her heartbroken sister and told her, "The Master is come, and calleth for thee." He was not impatient with her sorrow. Instead, He comes to help. I frequently suggest to those in sorrow that they get away from other people and quietly think and pray for a little while. Many people have told me that in that time they have felt the presence of God in a more definite way than ever before.

Above and beyond all things else, in time of sorrow over the passing of a loved one we should come to love and appreciate Christ the most. The story says Mary "arose and came quickly unto him." Surely to the One and only One who can assure eternal life for our loved ones and ourselves we should all want to come quickly— without further delay.

21. WILL WE KNOW EACH OTHER IN HEAVEN?

The Miracle of Raising Lazarus from the Dead

JOHN 11:1-46

IN COMPANY with Mary, Martha and a large number of other people, Jesus makes His way out to the cemetery where Lazarus was buried. Now we come to John 11:35, one of the most sublime verses in all the Bible. It contains only two words, but one could spend a long time considering the meaning of those two words: "Jesus wept." Why did He weep?

I once prepared a sermon on "The Sympathy of Christ" and I used those words as my text. It is certainly true that He understands our sorrows and enters into them with us. I still preach that sermon, but I had to get another text. Jesus did not weep over the death of Lazarus, because He knew that in a few moments Lazarus would be living again on this earth. Christ did not weep in sympathy with the sorrow of His friends, because in the raising of Lazarus their sorrow would be turned to joy.

I think the reason Christ wept that day was not because of the death of Lazarus, but rather because He felt it necessary to bring Lazarus back again to this earthly life.

In one of my first pastorates there lived one of the godliest women I have ever known. I visited her often and her sure and certain faith was a strengthening force in my own life. Especially was I impressed with her power in prayer and she was a great help to me in learning how to pray. Often when I had special requests for prayer I would go to her and we would pray together. Always I noted how careful she was to close her prayer asking God not to grant our request unless it was best.

One day I asked her why she was so careful at that point. She told me the story of her husband. He had a heart attack. The doctor came and did all he could but it was a losing battle. The doctor was listening to his heart and then quietly said, "He is gone." The children became almost hysterical and said, "Mama, pray, Mama, pray." Quickly she knelt and said, "Lord, bring him back to life." He opened his eyes, his breathing became regular, he lived for nine years more. But those nine years were for him so painful and unhappy that no less than a thousand times did she regret that God answered her prayer.

Often when someone dies we think how much better it would have been if that one could have lived. But we are not sure about that. Before we make up our minds or become bitter about some death, let us remember that we do not know all the facts. As the old song tells us:

> Not now, but in the coming years,
> It may be in the better land:
> We'll read the meaning of our tears,
> And there, some time we'll understand.

For a loved one to die is a heartbreaking experience. But for that one to live might be worse, very much worse. Who but God really knows? Thus let us not judge God until all the facts are before us.

WHY DIDN'T JESUS TELL US MORE ABOUT HEAVEN?

If we knew about the future life as Christ did, I am sure we would rejoice when one of our loved ones entered into it. Surely no one of us would be so selfishly cruel as to call one back from the City of God to the limitations and pains of this life.

That brings up the question, Why did not Jesus tell us more about Heaven? In the first place, there are no words in any language which can convey a true picture of the next life. Suppose you had the opportunity to talk with someone before he was born. Could you tell him what this life is like? Could you make a blind man understand what a sunset looks like? Could you tell a deaf man what great music sounds like?

St. Paul faced this situation and admitted our utter inability to understand the next life. He said, "Eye hath not seen, nor ear heard, neither have entered into the heart of man, the things which God hath prepared for them that love him" (I Cor. 2:9). I have often wondered why those who came back from the grave did not tell their experiences. I think the answer is they could not because of the total limitations of our language and understanding.

Another reason why I think Jesus did not tell us more of Heaven is that it would have utterly spoiled this life for us. I remember how long and dull the days before Christmas were when I was a child. Along in October I would begin looking at the mail-order catalogue and making up a list of all the things I was going to get. It was hard to wait for that blessed morning when Santa Claus would come.

Suppose you call your child to dinner. On his plate are spinach, carrots, meat and the other things he should eat. Then sitting beside his plate is a beautiful strawberry shortcake, covered with whipped cream. It's mighty hard to eat spinach with strawberry shortcake right before you. In fact, most children just can't do it.

And if Christ had put the picture of Heaven within our hearts and in our sight, could we bear to live on this earth? Knowing that other life, would it not cause us to weep even more to call one of our loved ones back to this life? Surely death is not a monster to be feared. It is the greatest blessing God has prepared for us.

But Christ felt it necessary to call Lazarus back. So He said to those sisters, "Take ye away the stone." He could have moved that stone with just a word. Instead, He required them to use their strength. God's miracles are not for the lazy. We must use our strength and do our part and then He does the rest. Prayer is never a substitute for the sweat of your brow.

Now notice that Christ says, "Father, I thank thee that thou hast heard me." What a marvelous lesson in prayer! We quickly come to ask, but how rarely do we come back to God to thank Him for hearing.

HE WAS STILL LAZARUS ON THE OTHER SIDE

At the grave Jesus said, "Lazarus, come forth." Those words reveal to us three great truths concerning life after death:

(1) Lazarus was living independently of the physical body he had on earth. That means that our physical bodies are not essential to our continued life. Many have the idea that there will come a resurrection of our bodies from the grave and we will live in them again.

But St. Paul clearly points out that "flesh and blood cannot inherit the kingdom of God." Our bodies go back to dust. Death means that we are released from this body we now have and we are given a spiritual body which will not be under the physical laws as our present bodies are. (Read I Corinthians 15.)

A mother whose baby had died asked me if the child will grow up in Heaven. Certainly there is growth in Heaven, but since we do not have physical bodies there we do not experience the physical growth we know here. After the death of his son, Calvin Coolidge inscribed on the flyleaf of a book these words: "To Edward K. Hall, in recollection of his son and my son, who have the privilege by the grace of God to be boys through all eternity."

(2) Those on the other side can hear those on this side. When Jesus called, Lazarus heard. I strongly believe there have been communications between people on each side of the grave. Heaven is not nearly so far away as we might suppose.

(3) Though our bodies are different, we are the same people on the other side as we are on this side. Jesus said, "Lazarus." Though he had died, he was still Lazarus.

He said, "Thy brother shall rise again." He was their brother on this side; he was still their brother on the other side. At home you may have a little one that you think of as "my child," and you are right. But you are just as right to think of that one of yours who may be in the Father's House as "my child."

On the authority of Christ, there is not the slightest doubt but that we will see and know and love each other again. This fact disturbed some people to the point that they asked Christ if people should marry several times, whose wife or husband would they be in the next life. He replied: "In the resurrection they neither marry, nor are given in marriage, but are as the angels of God in heaven" (Matt. 22:30). Marriage is a physical relationship and in Heaven we do not have physical bodies. The problems we think of in regard to the next life have all been worked out by God. We can trust Him to provide the right answers.

The important thing for us to know is that there is another life which is within the reach of every one of us. He said, "I am the resurrection, and the life: he that believeth in me, though he were dead, yet shall he live: and whosoever liveth and believeth in me shall never die." Then He added, "Believest thou this?" If you believe it, you will put your faith in Him as your Saviour and Lord.

22. NO SITUATION IS HOPELESS WITH GOD

*The Miracle of Raising the Daughter
of Jairus from the Dead*

MARK 5:21-43

———————

MANY PEOPLE believe in Christ because of His miracles. We agree with Nicodemus who said, "No man can do these miracles that thou doest, except God be with him" (John 3:2). Yet a lot of people try to explain away His miracles. Instead of feeding the five thousand, they say He just got the people to divide up with each other.

Some believe that the sick were not really sick but just thought they were, that the storm would have stopped anyway. But three times Jesus brought the dead back to life and that is a miracle we cannot explain away. Let's look at one of the instances.

We are told that Jairus, "one of the rulers of the synagogue," came to Jesus seeking help for his little daughter who was about to die. That is a very significant happening. The ones most opposed to Christ were the established church leaders. They had become set in their ways and they resisted any person who was the least bit different from them. That is even the case today. We become so set in our thinking that we refuse fellowship with someone who is different. One of the great temptations of church people is to become narrow and prejudiced and against anyone who is not in their own denomination.

No doubt this man, Jairus, had an open mind. Also, his child was sick and we never feel more desperately the need of help than when our children are in danger. Though Jairus was an outstanding leader, when he saw Christ "he fell at his feet." I like that. I know we can pray in any position, but I also know that we can pray best on our knees.

Jairus had the two things necessary to gain the power of God. First, he felt the need of help. As long as we feel sufficient unto ourselves, Christ will pass us by. "I can handle my life myself," we say. And as long as we say that, He will let us do it. When the boy wanted to leave his father's house and go to the far country, the father made no attempt to hold him. Christ does not force His way into any life. "Behold I stand at the door and knock," He says, but He waits for us to open the door. Through the sickness of his child Jairus became conscious of his need of Christ. Sometimes it is through some other need of life that we feel the need of help. But until we recognize the need for Him we will never have Him.

Second, Jairus had faith that Christ could do something about his need. He didn't say, "Come and try to heal my daughter." Christ has no time for triflers. He is not interested in one of us using Him as an experiment. He comes into our lives through the doorway of our belief. Jairus said, "I pray thee, come and lay thy hands on her, that she may be healed; and she shall live." That is faith; and when we believe, really believe that Christ can handle our situations, He will do it, but not before.

NO SITUATION IS HOPELESS

When Jairus, whose daughter was sick unto death, expressed his need of Christ and his faith in Christ's power, we read, "And Jesus went with him." It is hard to realize that the prayers of a man can change the plans of God, but such is the case. No doubt Jesus had other plans for that day, yet He changed those plans because of Jairus. Even our prayers today have the power to change the mind of God. Someone said, "Prayer changes things." There is no doubt about it. Prayer can even cause God to do things He would not have done without prayer. So Jesus turned aside to help this man who had come to him.

There is an important lesson to be learned right here. If God is willing to be interrupted, then we should not become bitter when our lives are interrupted. We remember that Job said, "My purposes are broken off" (Job 17:11).

As Jesus and Jairus made their way to the side of the sick child, there came messengers from the house saying, "Thy daughter is dead; why troublest thou the master any further?" But Jesus turned to the father and said, "Be not afraid, only believe." Our Lord puts no limit on the power of belief. Even by the side of death, faith is stronger. With Christ no person is hopeless, no situation is impossible. We give up hope too easily and too quickly.

There were a number of people following the Lord, but he allowed only Peter, James and John to go in with Him. We remember that He took those three on the Mount of Transfiguration with Him. Also, He took the same three a little further with Him in the Garden of Gethsemane. The presence of others who have faith is always a support. I've seen many people make a decision in a church service which they had not been able to make by themselves. Praying in the company of others who have faith is a great help to us.

In the house where death had come the people "wept and wailed greatly." Jesus rather impatiently asked, "Why make ye this ado?" Certainly He understands our sorrows and He knows how a heart can be broken. Surely no normal person can realize that a dear one has died and not have tears come into his eyes. Of course death brings sorrow. We would not have it otherwise.

On the other hand, in the presence of death a Christian should experience more than a pagan darkness. There is the faith of a glorious resurrection. The Christian faith is never more triumphant than in the presence of death. We never become ready to part with our loved ones. On the other hand, we rejoice in the realization that one we love has entered into the Father's House.

When O. Henry was dying, he whispered, "Turn up the light. I don't want to go home in the dark." In the presence of death Jesus is the light.

THE SUPPORT OF FAITH

When Jesus got to the home where the little girl had died He said, "The damsel is not dead, but sleepeth." This is the same word he used in reference to Lazarus. Though he had been buried for four days, Jesus said, "Our friend Lazarus sleepeth" (John 11:11). What a marvelous light that throws on the matter of death. It is not the cessation of life at all. Death simply means that one is living in another place.

Some of those present laughed at Christ, and He "put them all out." God is never willing to demonstrate His power to the cynical and the scornful. We blind ourselves to the glory of God by our unbelief. Into the room with Him Jesus brought His three disciples and the father and the mother. Because of their faith He was willing to let them see the miracle. Maybe, also, He felt the need of the support of their faith.

It means everything to us to have someone with us who believes in us and is pulling for us. On his eightieth birthday Henry Ford paid a lovely tribute to his wife. He said, "As I look back on my life, the unbroken happiness of my home and the confidence of my wife give me much more personal satisfaction than the building of a world-wide business organization. My wife believed in me so much that when many were doubting my early experiments, I called her 'The Believer'." It helps any of us to have with us a "believer." Even Christ needed it.

Standing by the side of that child who had died Jesus said, "Damsel, I say unto thee, rise." I have often wondered if people on the other side of life know anything that is happening on this side. I can't say, but I do know that Jesus could be heard by one on the other side. When I am out of town, I often take up a telephone and call my home and talk with those who are there. Jesus knew how to call His Father's House and talk with those there.

The girl who was dead came back to life. She arose and walked, to the astonishment of those present. Now notice what Jesus did. He commanded that she be given something to eat. There are three very important things to recognize here. First, her eating would serve as a supreme proof that she was living again. We remember that He ate after His resurrection.

Second, in recognizing her need of something to eat He is recognizing the fact that even though man cannot live by bread alone, still he does need bread. Jesus knows of our physical needs and is ever ready to help us.

Third, Jesus was wonderfully helping that mother and father when He commanded that the child be fed. They had been through a great emotional strain. Now, to help them, Jesus gave them something to do. Go in the kitchen, fix some food and bring it. There is no better medicine for our emotions and nerves than to get busy.

Jesus did raise a girl from the dead. But even more wonderful is the fact that He can still work His mighty miracles today to help those who believe in Him and will ask His help.